I0544324

FIRE ON THE MOON

DECORAH SECURITY SERIES, BOOK #19

REBECCA YORK

RUTH GLICK WRITING AS REBECCA YORK

Published by Light Street Press
Copyright © 2019 by Ruth Glick
Cover design by Earthly Charms

This is a work of fiction. Names, characters, places, and incidents either are the
product of the author's imagination or are used fictitiously, and any resemblance to
actual persons, living or dead, business establishments, events, or locales is entirely
coincidental.

ISBN: 978-1-943191-21-5

1

Had she leaped into the middle of a family feud? Or was this her chance to heal a twenty-year-old rift between two brothers? Francesca Turner wasn't sure, but she knew that her dying father kept saying he wished he could see his older brother, Angelo, one more time.

She ached to grant that wish. But she wasn't foolish enough to break the rules and simply invite her uncle to visit. She wanted to see what he was like first, and so she'd done a little research and contacted him on the phone.

The call coming out of the blue must have startled him.

"This is little Francesca?" he asked, his voice skeptical and at the same time hopeful.

"Yes. But I'm not a little girl anymore."

"It's been so long." His tone took on a note of urgency. "Where are you? Is your dad okay? Can I come and see you?"

"You know it's complicated. Why don't I come down there, and we'll talk first."

"Of course. Wonderful. I'll send you the air fare. Just give me a few days to finish some important business."

She'd agreed, and now here she was pulling into the driveway of his place in Naples, Florida—in what looked like a very plush neighborhood.

She hadn't told Dad about the trip. It was a secret—until she could be sure everything was okay.

There was a fence around the property. And when she pressed the buzzer on a post beside the high gate, she could see a camera inspecting her through the side window of her rental. Then a disembodied voice asked her to state her name and date of birth.

She blinked. That was what they always asked when you were calling to make a doctor's appointment—to double-check it was really you. The request from her uncle was like a little jolt from a stun gun, and she wondered if she'd made a serious mistake coming down here.

She looked behind her, wondering if she should just back up and return to the airport. Then she told herself she was over-reacting.

When the gate swung inward, she proceeded up a curving driveway bordered by lush foliage you'd only see indoors back home in Massachusetts. Among the green leaves were low plantings of bright impatiens and begonias that had long since been killed off by frost in New England.

The house had been invisible from the street, but as she rounded a bend, her jaw dropped. The white stucco structure sparkling in the tropical sun was the size of a small apartment building, but a lot more stylish, with shady verandas, a huge second-story balcony, a four-car garage and a front door that looked like it had been stolen from a Spanish castle.

As soon as she parked her rental Hyundai in the brick-paved circular drive, the massive door opened, and a short, dark-haired man wearing a bright Hawaiian shirt stepped out. He looked so much like her father that her breath caught. Well, she corrected herself, like Dad had looked before he'd gotten sick. But the prominent nose, the deep-set eyes and the wavy dark hair were the same.

As she climbed out of the car, he hurried to the driver's side, seeming a little nervous, and she suspected that he was wondering how to act, now that she'd arrived.

"Honey, you're all grown up. And you've turned into a beauty like your momma."

Mom had died a couple of years ago, and Francesca still missed her.

"I'm sorry you didn't want to stay with me," Uncle Angelo continued, then looked like he wished he hadn't said it.

"I didn't want to put you to any trouble," she answered cautiously. Really, she had good reason to keep some distance between them.

"Well, I'm so glad you came. Come in. Come in. You must be worn out from your trip."

She studied his tanned face. Now that the greetings were over, she saw that his features were drawn and his eyes darted around the garden before coming back to her.

"What's wrong?" she asked.

"Nothing. Nothing. I'm just trying to finalize a business deal." He led her into an entrance foyer as large as Dad's living room back home, then through to a covered veranda. The view swept down to the Gulf, where she saw a wrought iron fence blocking direct access to the beach. She might have asked him if he ever went down there, but she didn't want to start off this reunion by bringing up his security concerns.

Searching for something to say, she murmured, "This is a beautiful setting."

"Yes. I was lucky to find the property."

At one side of the seating area was an alfresco kitchen, where he opened the fridge and brought out a bright red plastic pitcher.

"Fresh-squeezed orange juice," he said. "A perfect welcome to

Florida. And some little sandwiches. Chicken salad. Tuna. Ham and cheese. Egg salad. I had my housekeeper make them before she went home for the day. What's your pleasure?"

It was hard to focus on the question because she was having trouble taking in everything. Before he'd started getting nostalgic, her father had called Uncle Angelo a selfish bastard, and this man was all solicitude. Or maybe he was working overtime to show he'd changed since the good old days.

She put two triangular sandwiches on her plate—tuna and ham and cheese.

"Try the orange juice," her uncle urged. "The oranges are from the trees right over there."

Dutifully she picked up her glass and took a swallow. "It's good."

"How come you decided to contact me?" Angelo asked.

"Dad's not doing too well. He's had Parkinson's disease for a couple of years, and it's gotten worse."

"Oh no. I'm so sorry. What about your mom?"

"She passed away."

"So you'll be alone in the world when your father dies."

She nodded.

"All the more reason it's good you phoned me. We gotta keep in touch." He reached into his pocket and produced a small velvet bag. Opening it, he took out what looked like an antique gold locket.

"This was your grandmother's. Dante's and my mom's. From the old country." Dante had been her dad's name before he changed it.

She stared at the piece. It looked old and valuable. "I've never seen it."

"Well, I've had it for years, but I don't have a daughter. I'd be so happy if you'd take it."

She fingered the scrollwork on the front. "I . . ."

"Put it on. and wear it with pride," he urged.

4

She hesitated, then slipped the heavy gold chain over her head and felt the locket settle against her chest.

"Beautiful," he breathed. "It looks like it was made for you."

Since he obviously wanted to get closer to her, maybe it was the right time to ask, "What happened between you and my father?"

He shifted in his seat, looking like he wished someone would come and rescue him.

"You know how it is when you get mad at someone and can't let it go?"

"Actually, no."

Before he could elaborate, a flicker of movement down by the beach caught her attention. Two large tough-looking men dressed in knit shirts and jeans were coming across the sand toward the fence.

As Angelo turned to see what had caught her attention, he made a strangled sound.

"Oh no. Not now."

"What?"

"Come on. Quick." He turned and took her arm.

Dragging her up, he propelled her toward the house. Inside, he headed back to the front hall and opened the double doors to the coat closet. He swept the hanging clothing aside and pressed the edge of the back wall. A door slid open, and he shoved her into a dark, closed space. "Don't make a sound if you don't wanna get dragged into this."

Quickly he closed the door, and his footsteps receded.

It had all happened so fast that she hardly had time to absorb his words. But as the implications slammed into her, she started to shake.

Voices drifted toward her from the back of the house.

"Don't try it, old man," a threatening baritone advised.

She heard something that sounded like a fist slamming into

flesh, and someone made a gagging sound. She had to assume one of the men had hit her uncle.

God, if she could only call 911 and ask for help from the police. But her phone was in her purse, and it was still on the table on the veranda.

Oh no. Her uncle had shoved her into this hidden space at the back of the closet, but the men had surely seen her pocketbook and knew she was here.

One of the men was speaking again. "You think you can go up against the boss?"

"I'm not." Her uncle answered, his voice sounding high and thin.

"What would you call it?"

"I was going to let him in on it."

"Sure."

There was a pause in the threatening conversation, and she held her breath, waiting for what might come next.

Not more words, only another cry of pain.

She hardly knew her uncle, but it was torture standing here in the dark listening to him being hurt. And there was nothing she could do. If she went out there, they'd just beat her up, too. Or maybe they'd kill a witness.

Could she get out of the closet and make it to the street? She wasn't even sure how the hidden door worked, and if she tried to open it, the noise might give her away.

"You got one more chance." The murderous voice threatened from the back of the house.

There was a long pause. It was followed by two little popping sounds that might have been firecrackers. Under the circumstances she was pretty sure they had come from a handgun.

2

Francesca stood paralyzed inside the hidden space at the back of the closet. One of those tough-looking men had shot her uncle. Or was that true? She hadn't seen anything, only heard the voices and what she thought was gunfire.

The question was settled when one of the invaders spoke.

"We gotta get rid of the body."

"And we gotta find the girl. We both saw her with him on the patio."

"You think she's got any information?"

The second man laughed. "She's got information that we just offed her uncle. You put him in the trunk. I'll start looking for her."

"The old bastard's heavy. I'm not gonna do it by myself."

"Okay. Okay. You bring the car around."

Her heart blocked her windpipe. Could she get out while they were removing her uncle's body? She wanted to sneak out, but what if one of the guys saw her? If he did, she knew she was a dead woman for sure because they'd already killed one person.

They'd wanted something from Uncle Angelo, and she didn't even know what it was.

She heard their heavy breathing as they came into the hall.

"Wait a minute," one of them said.

"What for?"

Above the roaring in her ears, she heard the other one answer, "The coat closet. Maybe she hid in there."

As she stood in complete darkness, clenching her teeth to keep them from chattering, she heard the sound of the coats being swished aside again.

When a hand pounded against the wall, her heart stopped for a moment—then started to thump so loudly that she was sure the man would hear it.

And if she fainted, he'd hear her fall to the floor.

Stiffening her legs, she forced herself to stand rigidly in place, afraid to even lean backwards.

She wasn't sure how long she waited there, listening to him rummaging around. Each second stretched into minutes as she prayed that he wouldn't figure out that there was a hidden compartment at the back of the closet.

Finally, she heard footsteps withdraw and dared to slowly let the breath she'd been holding trickle out of her lungs. Still she waited for long moments before daring to move. She hadn't had a chance to examine this space. Now she took a step back and then another until she softly bumped into a horizontal surface. Maybe the space was four feet deep. And when she walked from one side to the other, she found it was perhaps six feet wide— which meant that she could lie down if she wanted. She also discovered that there was a set of shelves to her right. It held a few bottles of water and a flashlight. Was there a crack where the light might show? Afraid to find out, she held the light in her hand like a club, thinking how ineffective that would be against men with guns.

Letting herself slide down the wall, she pressed her back

against the hard surface, and drew her knees up to her chin. When the bad guys didn't find her, she could get out of here and run.

There were noises coming from other parts of the house—probably from the men searching. Sometime later, she heard them talking.

"No go?"

"She's got to be in here somewhere."

"I think she got away somehow."

"Not likely. With the body gone, we've got time to keep searching for her."

Because her watch lacked a lighted dial, there was no way to judge time. Was it dark out there? All she knew was that she had stepped from a sunny day in Naples, Florida, into hell.

———

With the long-legged strides of an athlete, Zane Marshall ran along the beach. As a werewolf, he would have preferred to run in his animal form, but there were too many people in the mansions that lined this exclusive stretch of sand. The wolf would have to wait for a trip to one of the area's nature preserves or state parks where he could slip in after the gates were closed.

He'd come down to Naples, Florida, on a job. A hysterical homeowner named Chuck Cruise, who had heard about the track record of Decorah Security in the paranormal field, had called Frank Decorah with an urgent plea. Strange things were happening on his property, and he was convinced his home was under attack from a malevolent spook trying to drive him away. He was desperate for Frank to send an agent down right away. Zane had been glad to take the assignment because he'd been feeling restless in his usual routine. When he arrived, he listened to a long recitation about peculiar lights and threatening sounds coming and going in the night. He told Cruise he'd get to the bottom of it and set hidden cameras around the property. The surveillance had paid off. He'd gotten footage proving that the spook was really a vengeful neighbor who was trying to scare the spit out of the Decorah client. The perpetrator was angry about trees that screened both properties from the road. Cruise had paid his garden service to cut then down, and the neighbor had retaliated. Zane figured out what was going on but had almost gotten shot in the process. After that he'd decided he was due a little R and R in the sunshine state, and Frank Decorah had given him a week off.

The firm sand of the beach was the perfect place for a man to run. And his mind was free to range where it would. He'd told himself he needed a vacation, and yet he knew it was more than that. He couldn't shake the feeling that something was waiting for him in this place—something unknown. Part of him wanted to flee back to Maryland. And part of him was damned if he was going to try and outrun his destiny.

As he'd passed a row of palatial houses, he'd wondered who owned them. One place in particular had caught his interest because of the fencing around the property. What kind of person would buy a house along the shore and then block access to the water?

Previously he'd seen an old guy, usually wearing a Hawaiian shirt, standing out on the patio and scanning the beach or perhaps staring out into the blue water. Now he could see two other men dressed in knit shirts and jeans on the veranda. They were big, tough looking guys poking around inside the storage boxes that served as part of the seating and leaving the cushions where they'd scattered onto the veranda. One of them picked up something Zane couldn't see and stuffed it into his pocket.

As Zane watched, he was unable to tamp down his detective's curiosity. Something was out of pattern here, and he'd like to know what.

He could have assumed that these men were friends of the old guy, but they weren't treating his property very kindly.

He jogged farther down the beach, then cut to the right, away from the ocean, onto the grounds of a nearby house. Ducking into the tropical vegetation, he made his way back toward the fence in time to see one of the newcomers open the gate and step onto the sand. He shaded his eyes, as though he were trying to see if anybody was observing him and his companion before heading back to the veranda. It was getting dark now, and it looked like they were planning something. Perhaps the wolf could get close enough to figure out what.

Francesca wasn't sure how long she had stayed hidden. It seemed like years, but she knew it could only have been a few hours.

Was it safe to come out? She wished she knew. She hadn't heard any noises in the house for a long time, but that didn't prove anything. They could be lying low, waiting for her to think it was okay to make a run for it.

She was still trying to decide what to do when she detected an acrid smell. It took a few moments for her to realize it was smoke, not the welcoming scent of a campfire but the nasty tang of burning domestic materials.

Oh Lord, the house must be on fire. And she had to assume the two men had done it.

She picked up the flashlight and leaped to the front of her hiding place, shining the light over the vertical surface, but she could see nothing that looked like a latch. Was it something that worked by pressure. She tucked the flashlight under her arm and slid her hands against the wall, trying to find some mechanism that would open the hidden door. Again nothing.

As the smoke seeped into the space behind the closet, she struggled to keep from coughing and giving herself away.

Although panic threatened to cut off logical thought, she knew that she didn't have much time to save herself. She'd read somewhere that you had about three minutes to get out of a burning house because the furnishings and the building materials were so flammable.

In the distance she could hear the wail of sirens. The fire department was on the way, although it would be too late to save her. She had to get out of the house, but she couldn't escape the compartment at the back of the closet by the way she'd come in. That meant there had to be another exit. Again she shined the flashlight over the walls, this time focusing on the remaining three. In one of the short walls, she saw a small chink at the corner. When she pressed on it, the panel slid back. She wanted to dash out, but what if one of the killers was waiting on the other side? Cautiously she peered through and saw a long narrow passageway. Behind her more smoke seeped into the room, and it felt like the walls were getting hot. With no other choice, she stepped into the tunnel and ran along the passage. It ended in another blank wall, but this time when she shined the light over it, she detected the same kind of crack she'd seen before. If she stepped through, would one of the killers be standing there?

The crackling of flames behind her warned that she couldn't' delay. Clenching her teeth, she pressed on the latch, then held her breath as the wall slid open. It was almost dark outside, but as far as she could see, she was alone, staring into dense tropical foliage. With no other choice, she stepped out beside a bush with green and yellow variegated leaves. She seemed to be at the side of the house. And as she recalled the view of the mansion from the circular drive, she thought she must also be at the back side of the garage.

Moving cautiously through the bushes and flower beds, she peered out and saw the fence. Could she get to it? Would the gate be locked? Or had the men left it open for their own escape.

They must be watching for her. Or maybe they had decided it was too dangerous to stay with a fire truck coming.

She thanked God when she saw the gate was open a sliver. She made a dash for it. Before she reached it, one of the killers stepped from behind a clump of bushes. When he raised his arm, she saw the gun in his hand.

3

"Got 'ya."

The man pulled a gun, but before he could fire, a large dog sprang from behind a palm tree and leaped on the thug. The gun discharged as he went down, but his aim was wild.

Still, the noise brought his partner running. The man rolled on the ground, crying out as the dog chomped on his arm. The other man was trying to get a shot at the dog, but there was no way to do it with his friend and the animal shifting positions.

Francesca didn't know where the animal had materialized from or why it had come to her rescue. But she saw it give one last chomp to the thug's arm before suddenly leaping on the other man and knocking him to the ground.

The killer screamed and dropped his weapon. Both men were on the sand now, neither of them equipped to shoot the dog.

Taking the opportunity to escape, she slipped into the crowd of people who had gathered between the house and the Gulf, their gazes glued to the fire. As far as she could tell, none of them had seen her or the animal attack. For a split second she considered running up to one of them and explaining what had happened.

Then she tried to think logically. This had started—with a shooting. But she hadn't seen it. Was she going to sound crazy if she tried to explain? Or would the cops believe her? Wasn't the person who found a murder victim the prime suspect? Maybe she had shot her uncle and started the fire to cover it up.

Of course, she had another problem. She'd been so cautious about coming down here because her father had always implied that her uncle was a dangerous character who ran with bad company. She'd prayed he had changed. Apparently not. Scumbags had killed him. Well, she hadn't seen it, but she had heard what they were saying. It sounded like he was in an illegal deal, he'd tried to double-cross someone they'd called "the boss," and he'd been executed.

Those conflicting thoughts followed her down the beach as she took off running. Afraid to look back, she kept trying to put distance between herself and the murder scene. Just as she'd decided to slow down, she heard footsteps rapidly catching up with her.

Oh Lord, one of the bad guys had gotten away from the dog and was about to grab her.

She tried to put on a burst of speed, but she was already exhausted.

"Wait."

She struggled on.

"Wait, I saw what happened. I want to help you."

Saw what? The fire? The gun? The dog? Still afraid to trust anyone, she looked toward the houses that ran along the shoreline, wondering if she could slip between them and get away. The movement slowed her and the man who had called out put a hand on her shoulder.

"Stop running."

The hand sent a zing of reaction through her, but she simply couldn't give in to it, not after everything that had happened. When she tried to wrench herself away, she stumbled. She would have landed in the sand, but the man caught her, pulling her against his body. He felt solid and well built—well muscled without being a weight lifter type, and his arms around her were reassuring in a way she couldn't articulate. He could have easily locked her in his grasp, but he wasn't holding her tightly. The knowledge that she was free to step away from him kept her standing in his embrace, comforted by the sturdy feel of him.

As his hands soothed over her shoulders and down her arms, she struggled to stop trembling.

"It's okay. I can help," Zane said again, hearing the thick quality of his voice. His natural impulse had been to help a victim. Yet as he cradled this woman in his arms, he was feeling a lot more than the need to offer aid.

She didn't answer, and he understood why she couldn't rely on him—or anybody else right now. She'd escaped from a burning building, only to see two men try to capture her. They'd been taken down by what looked like a large dog that had appeared out of nowhere. She didn't know the dog was a wolf, and the wolf was him. And he couldn't tell her he was the one who had rescued her. He wouldn't give away that information to anyone he didn't trust implicitly.

He'd left the men rolling on the ground, bleeding and nursing major bites. And he'd made sure some of those bites were in their hands so that firing a gun would have been almost impossible. As a wolf, that had been the best he could do to disable the thugs without killing them. Then he'd found his running shorts, shirt and shoes where he'd left them in the bushes and changed back to human form, pushing through the transformation before taking off after the woman.

She raised her head, looking dazed, and maybe that gave him his best chance.

"Let me help you."

She focused on his face, and he knew she was trying to get a sense of him beyond the superficial exterior of a lean, fit guy in his early thirties who had come dashing down the sand after her when nobody else had turned away from the fire.

He tried to project honesty and calm.

"Who are you?" she asked in a shaky voice.

Your life mate. The answer leaped into his mind, stunning him. Yet he pushed the crazy notion down into the depths of his soul as soon as it had surfaced.

She spoke while he was still feeling dizzy with the possibility of truth.

"Why would you help me? What's this to you?" her question only reinforced the emotions clanging through him.

By an effort of will, he kept his gaze steady. He couldn't deal with the life-changing idea that had slapped him in the face, but he knew he had to cope with the immediate situation.

"It's my job. My name is Zane Marshall. I'm a private detective. I work for an agency called Decorah Security."

"I never heard of it."

"We're in Maryland, but I came down here on an assignment, and when I was finished, I decided to stay in Naples for a couple of days. I was running on the beach, and I saw something happening up at your house."

"Not my house—my uncle's," she said, giving him a piece of information he hadn't previously possessed.

"You live with him?"

"No. I just came down from . . . outside Boston."

He could see it had taken an effort to get that much out. When she wavered on unsteady legs, he pulled her toward him, holding her in his arms, not tightly but enough to keep her upright.

"Were you trapped in there? He asked.

"No, I was hiding."

"From those men?"

"Yes."

She said no more. She must have been holding herself together by force of will. Now she started to shake.

He gathered her closer, and he could feel her fighting tears.

"You're okay," he murmured. "Everything's going to be okay." Hoping it wasn't a lie, he added. "But you're too exposed out here on the beach. We should get inside.'"

She nodded against his shoulder but didn't move. "Those men?"

"A big dog went after them."

"Why?"

A glib answer came to his lips. "Maybe he's a guard dog— trained to respond to an attack."

Perhaps that satisfied her for the moment. When he turned slightly, he felt her stiffen her legs.

"Come on. I've got an Airbnb just a few hundred yards down the beach." When she made no move to go with him, he repeated, "You're too exposed. You need to get out of the open. Before they come searching for you," he added, although he was pretty sure that wasn't going to happen anytime soon.

She shuddered, then turned and looked back the way they'd come, seeing the black smoke rising into the sky where a house had been. There was no sign of the men—or the dog.

She made a small sound of distress, and he knew the smoke had reinforced the urgency of his words.

It seemed that he had to say everything to her twice. "Come on."

"Where?"

"My place."

She hesitated, then took a step in the direction she'd been running. Once she had gotten moving, she kept putting one foot in front of the other, looking like a dazed passenger astonished to be walking away from a plane crash. He moved in beside her, then slowly pulled her against his side so that he was partially supporting her. Luckily his short-term rental wasn't far. It was on the same stretch of beach but definitely not as grand as the one that had just burned down. He took her to the side of the house on a stepping-stone path to the front door where he retrieved the key from a hiding place in the shrubbery, unlocked the door, and ushered her into a small foyer and beyond to a great room. Like most of the houses along the Gulf, the wall facing the beach had large windows. But here there was no fence obstructing the view. She looked for a place to sit and dropped into a high-backed contoured chair.

He closed a set of drapes, then stepped into the downstairs master suite where he quickly pulled on a pair of sweatpants. After a stop in the kitchen he handed her a glass of water. "Sorry I don't have anything stronger." He didn't add that a werewolf's system couldn't abide anything stronger than herbal tea.

He sat on a matching chair opposite her, trying not to look like he was studying her—that he wasn't taking in every detail from her blond hair to her blue eyes to her slender figure, covered by only a sundress.

She took a swallow of water, then set the glass down on a round glass-topped table.

"Feeling any better?

"Yes."

"What happened—exactly?"

"What did you see?" she countered.

She was still being cautious, and he couldn't fault her for that.

"I've been running on the beach every day since I got here. Most days I saw an older man out on the patio of the house where you were."

"My uncle."

"Then, this afternoon, you were out there with him. I hadn't seen you before, and I slowed down."

"Why?"

"He'd always been alone before. Not long after the two of you came outside, I saw two thuggish-looking men come up along the beach and break through the gate."

"Yes."

He was glad to focus on business instead of examining his reaction to her. "Who were they?"

"I don't know. Uncle Angelo saw them coming and dragged me to the front hall closet. There was a hidden space behind the back wall, and he pushed me inside and closed the panel. Then I heard them questioning him in the living room."

"About what?"

"I'm not sure. They were being rough with him. It sounded like they wanted something. I don't know what because they all seemed to know what they were talking about, so there wasn't much information exchanged. When he wouldn't cooperate . . . they beat on him. Then . . ." She stopped and took a shaky breath. "They shot him."

He hadn't heard anything. Or perhaps he had on some almost subliminal level. "You're sure?"

"I heard what sounded like gunshots." She shuddered. "Then they were talking about getting rid of his body."

She was watching to see how he reacted to her story of violence and murder. He put on his best professional face. He'd already decided when he didn't see the old man come out of the house after the fire had started that the guy was dead or injured, and this was just confirmation.

"You said you were a private detective," she blurted. "Can I hire you?"

As soon as she said it, panic flashed across her face. "Oh my God. I just realized, I don't have my purse. Either it burned up in the fire, or those men took it when they took away my uncle's body."

"How do you know they took away the body?"

"They talked about putting it in the trunk of their car."

She reached for the glass of water and took a gulp, then slumped down in the chair.

He wanted to cross the room, scoop her up and cradle her in his lap, but he stayed where he was. "I already said I'd help you."

"What does that mean?"

He focused on the immediate problem. "Keeping you safe while we figure out who killed your uncle and why."

She dipped her head. "I'm sure a bodyguard is expensive."

"Don't worry about that. Frank Decorah, the head of my agency, has a fund for clients in need."

"You mean charity," she shot back.

"Don't put it that way."

"How would you put it?" she challenged.

"That the most important thing right now is to keep those men from killing you."

Her skin turned a shade paler.

Pressing his advantage, he asked, "What else can you tell me?"

"Let me think about it."

He clenched his fists at his sides. He'd offered to save her life, and she wasn't willing to help him? Maybe she was too strung out to think straight. Or maybe she had something to hide. Like was she part of some illegal scheme that had gone bad? He hated to think that was true.

"How about your name," he tried.

"My name," she murmured. "Right, I'm Francesca."

He waited for a last name, but it wasn't forthcoming.

Trying to make the best of her reticence, he said, "You've been through a pretty bad experience. Why don't you get some sleep? We can talk about it in the morning."

"Yes. Thanks."

He noted her grateful look, but he was pretty sure she wanted to put some distance between them. Because he was coming across as too intense? Or because she was still sorting out her own problems?

"Do you want something to eat first?"

"I don't think I could."

It was hard not to press her with more questions—like for example, do you want to call the police? And if not, why not? Instead he led her upstairs and showed her to one of the bedrooms he wasn't using.

Probably she didn't want to sleep in her sundress. And if she took it off, was it one of those models where the bra was built in? He yanked his mind away from that train of thought.

"Let me bring you something to sleep in." He backed away and headed downstairs to the master bedroom. He came back with one of his tee shirts and set it on the dresser. "You can borrow this. There should be toilet articles in the bathroom."

"I hate to be putting you in this position," she said, looking relieved that he was going to give her some space.

"I volunteered," he answered, then waited a beat to see if she'd part with any other information. When she didn't, he turned and left the room, hearing her shut and lock the door behind him.

He pictured her in there, taking off the sundress. She'd leave her panties on before she pulled his tee shirt over her head. He pictured it falling against her skin, pictured the way her breasts would fill out the front.

With a silent curse, he turned away and started down the stairs again. He had always had an easy time with women. There was something about the animal nature of the werewolf that attracted them. He'd enjoyed a number of relationships, although he'd always made it clear that he wasn't interested in anything long-term. In his early twenties, he'd figured he had plenty of time before he had to settle down. As he'd approached thirty, he'd felt a certain unease, like he was going to fall into something he wasn't ready for. Still, he'd told himself he had choices. That had given him a false sense of security, and he hadn't been prepared for his reaction to this particular damsel in distress.

He was aroused by a woman he couldn't trust, and that wasn't doing anything for his mood.

Doggedly he forced himself to focus on practicalities. Probably she'd be hungry by morning. The werewolf diet wasn't exactly typical breakfast food. He was happiest with meat. But he supposed the house was well enough stocked so that she could find something that worked for her in the morning. He might have gone out to pick up some supplies, but he wasn't going to leave her alone, in case something else happened—or in case she tried to slip away when his back was turned.

That last thought made his stomach clench.

But she wouldn't, he told himself. Her uncle had been murdered, just after she'd come to see him. She had no money and no ID. And she definitely had something to hide; otherwise, she would have wanted to call the cops.

Yeah, he thought, a great reason for a woman to stay with him.

He didn't even know if her real name was Francesca. And she conveniently didn't have identification.

He'd seen she was in trouble and jumped in to save her. Now he couldn't help wondering if he was harboring a criminal. Or was he looking for an excuse to keep himself from bonding with her?

Bonding? Was he letting his thoughts carry him that far?

Yeah, he was, and he didn't exactly like it.

The house he'd rented had been outfitted with surveillance equipment because there had been some robberies in the area. He'd thought he didn't need it, but now he was glad it had been installed. Turning on the monitor screens, he checked the cameras that gave various views of the property, then set the alarm that would alert him if anybody was sneaking up on the house.

He left it on and retrieved some raw steak from the fridge which he cut into several chunks. Turning on the TV, he found a local news outlet and ate while he watched a breathless account of the fire, complete with video of the firefighters' futile efforts to put out the blaze, although their quick efforts were credited with saving the houses on either side of the property. Arson was suspected, and so far there was no evidence of any fatalities. According to property records, the owner of the house was Angelo Lucci. And Francesca had also given the uncle that first name. Was her last name the same? Or were they even related? She could even be his mistress.

No, that last thought was going too far. He hated doubting everything she'd told him, but her reluctance to give him any details made it impossible to trust her.

Neighbors were talking about Angelo Lucci. Apparently he'd kept to himself, and of course he'd taken the unusual step of literally walling himself off. Nobody knew him well, although he hadn't caused any trouble as far as anyone could recall. It was like the amazed reaction when someone turned out to be a serial killer, and everyone was shocked to learn he had a secret life.

Zane sighed. With the alarm on, maybe he could afford to get a little sleep after he'd done some more investigation, but he'd better be ready for action at any time.

He broke off his search for local information and sent an e-mail to Frank Decorah explaining what was happening and what he knew. Maybe his best bet would be to take Francesca to Decorah headquarters while he investigated the case.

After the e-mail to Decorah, he went back to digging for anything he could find on Francesca. She had said she had come down here from the Boston area. If she was on the up and up, there might be an easy way to find some stuff out.

He got into the Facebook account he rarely used and put in the name Francesca Lucci—and got nothing. Same with Instagram and Twitter.

Either she didn't use social media, or she was posting under some other name.

4

F rancesca hugged her arms around her shoulders as she
turned in a circle, inspecting the bedroom.

Zane Marshall had said he worked for a detective agency and
had come down to Naples for a job. Just to do a little checking
on his story, she opened drawers and inspected the closet in her
bedroom. It was clear that the room wasn't occupied by anyone
on a regular basis, which might or might not prove anything. She
had heard him go downstairs, and maybe she might have done a
little more snooping if she hadn't been sure she'd get caught at it.
He had a way of listening and looking that made her think of an
animal on the hunt. He'd told her he wanted to help her, but she
had gotten the impression that he'd make a formidable enemy,
and she didn't want to do anything to get on his bad side.

At the same time she knew she was attracted to him, which
didn't make any sense because she'd never been the kind of
woman who dated men she considered dangerous. And that's
how she'd describe him.

All that rattled around in her head as she lay in bed, wearing
his tee shirt. It felt like much too intimate a thing to do. But she

couldn't sleep in her sundress and she certainly wasn't going to lie here naked except for her panties.

She was sure she wouldn't sleep, not just because she was alone with a strange man—a man she couldn't figure out. She'd been through too much with her uncle, the thugs, and the fire. She reached to clasp the locket her uncle had given her. He'd said it was a cherished family possession. He'd wanted her to have it, and now he was dead. Could she ask Dad about it? She winced. That would mean having to tell him the whole horrible story of coming down here.

Her mind kept turning over the day's events, but she was so wrung out that she did finally drift off. She woke with a start a few hours after the sun came up, yanked from a sensual dream with a dark-haired man whose face she couldn't see. But she knew it had been Zane Marshall, the man who had rescued her and brought her to his house.

And now her dreams had turned him into a lover? She clenched her teeth, intent on banishing the implications. The dream didn't make it any easier to face her host.

She knew at once that there was no use lying in bed any longer. She'd only be hiding from whatever was going to happen today. She would either have to trust Zane Marshall or get out of his hair. As soon as that thought struck, she felt a powerful pang of loss. She wanted to stay with him. And then what?

She'd still be in trouble. Longing to give her father the gift of connecting with his only brother, she'd found Angelo Lucci's number and called him. But she should have stifled the impulse. It had been stupid to get tangled up with him again after all these years. She should have remembered all the negative things Dad had said about his brother before he'd gotten sick and started obsessing about his old life.

Unwilling to face Zane yet, she spent some time in the shower, then wished she had something to wear besides the sundress and sandals that had seemed so right for Florida. She didn't even have the jacket she'd worn on the plane because that had burned up last night.

Finally she knew it was past the time for delay. When she came downstairs, she found him sitting in one of the living room chairs with his long legs up on a large footstool. Sometime in the night he'd changed into jeans and a pullover shirt.

She studied him as she reached the first floor. It looked like he'd spent the night there. And he was a lot less worse for wear than she was. On the other hand, nobody had tried to kill him yesterday.

"How are you?" he asked, making the question casual.

"I wouldn't say I'm great," she answered honestly. "Maybe a cup of coffee would help."

"I don't drink coffee."

"Really?" She looked around the kitchen and spotted a Keurig on the counter. "There are probably pods for this."

"I guess. I haven't looked."

"What are you going to drink?"

"Herbal tea."

She tried not to wrinkle her nose as she turned away and found a basket of pods.

"There's no milk," he warned.

"I get by with sugar," she answered, eying the nearby basket of packets.

While she fixed herself a mug of Donut Shop, he used the hot-water dispenser at the sink to fill another mug and put in a tea bag that smelled like ginger.

She knew she was stalling as she opened the pantry and then the fridge looking for something to eat. The only thing in the fridge was meat.

When she found a box of crackers in a cabinet, she pulled it out and bit into one. It was just on the edge of stale.

Looking up, she saw him watching her. For a long moment, neither of them moved, and it seemed as though they were trying to share secret information that neither of them wanted to speak. But staring at each other wasn't going to cut it. She swallowed. This was decision time. She was in a hell of a fix, and she couldn't cope on her own.

She watched him watching her. "All right," she finally said.

"All right what?"

Her fingers tightened around the mug in her hand. "I guess you're thinking that any normal person would go to the police, but I can't do that because my father is in the witness protection program. He's been known as Glen Turner for the past eighteen years. Before that, he was in the mob in New Jersey."

The words came out in a rush. She felt her face flush and wanted to look away, but she kept her gaze steady, judging his reaction. When she didn't see condemnation in his eyes, she went on,

"As far as I know, he never killed anyone." She followed that observation with a nervous laugh. "I guess he beat some guys up when he was ordered to. But he was into robberies mostly. He got caught by the cops highjacking a truckload of cigarettes. Once they had him in custody, they used leverage against him. He ended up ratting out some of his friends because he didn't want to go to prison and leave me and my mom. He got into the witness protection program and also a training program where he became a plumber. We lived a middle-class life where nobody knew his real background."

Again Zane didn't interrupt, and she went on. "I was only eight when Dad went straight. I really don't even remember his old life. I just used to hear my parents talking about it, sometimes late at night when they thought I was asleep. They had to leave their whole family behind and take on new identities. Mom died a few years ago, and now Dad's got Parkinson's disease. It's gradually gotten worse, and he's in a nursing home. He's been talking about how much he missed his brother. And I decided to come down here and see if I could arrange a visit. I mean, when Dad's dead, he won't be in the program anymore. What harm could it do to let him see his brother one last time?

She gulped. "That's how I got myself into this mess."

She had dreaded admitting her shameful family background. Instead she felt as though a weight had been lifted off her shoulders. Even better, Zane Marshall hadn't told her he didn't want to get involved, and he hadn't thrown her out.

Still facing her, he said in a steady voice, "And shortly after you arrived, men came into the house, killed your uncle, and tried to kill you."

"Yes."

"And you don't know why?"

"I told you, I haven't had any contact with him since I was a little girl."

"Was your uncle in the mob, too?"

She set the mug on the counter. "I don't know. It wasn't like he and dad discussed their business where I could hear them."

"Your last name is Turner—like your dad's?"

"Yes."

"But before he went into the witness protection program, it was the same as your uncle's—Lucci?"

Her head jerked up. "How do you know his name?"

"TV coverage of the fire. After the house burned, it was all over the news last night."

She smacked her forehead. "Oh, right. It would be. Nothing like pictures of a house burned to the ground to generate interest."

"How did you know where to find him?"

She flushed slightly. "I used one of those online services that locates people."

He started to ask her another question, when a series of beeps interrupted him.

Cursing under his breath, he strode into the living room, opened a cabinet, and pulled out some kind of electronic device.

When he flicked a switch, a monitor screen came to life. It didn't seem to be showing any kind of program, just a static picture of some trash cans. He flicked the switch again, and the view changed. This time she saw the path that she'd come up with Zane when he'd led her off the beach. On the stepping-stones was a man creeping along the side of the house, gun in hand.

As she drew in a quick breath, Zane changed the scene again. This time she saw shrubbery and another armed man moving along at a crouch.

5

Zane hadn't known exactly what to expect, but he was always prepared for trouble. Now he second-guessed himself as he wondered what he should have done. Maybe take Francesca to a safer location?

But then he would have had to set up monitoring equipment.

Neither of these guys had a bandaged hand. They weren't the ones from last night. But they must be connected. Which meant the attack last night wasn't just a two-man show. Lucci must be important. Or maybe they were really after Francesca. Why had they stayed away all night and come around now? To give him a false sense of security? Or was there something more strategic involved? Maybe they'd figured that as long as he and Francesca stayed put, they could pick their time to attack. Or perhaps they'd been hoping he'd leave Francesca alone so they could swoop in.

All that zinged through his mind as he watched the men coming along either side of the house, toward the front. Probably there was another thug on the beach side.

He took her arm. "Come on."

"Where?" she asked, her voice high and wavery.

"Away."

He handed her his laptop. "Take this for me."

When she'd clutched the notebook-sized machine in her arms, he reached under his shirt and drew his own weapon from a holster at his belt. Francesca glanced at the semiautomatic as he led her quickly through a little hallway at the side of the kitchen before stopping at the door to the garage, He moved her to the side, out of the line of fire if anyone was waiting for them to emerge. With a rapid jerk, he pulled the door open with his left hand, his weapon in his right. Scanning the garage, he saw with relief that the area was clear. Just a dim, orderly space with his rented SUV parked inside.

He put his finger to his lips, then gestured toward the vehicle, which he'd pulled close to the door, glad that he'd taken the extra time to park it facing outward.

"Get in the back, and scrunch down on the floor," he whispered.

She had sense enough not to argue as he quietly closed the door behind her.

Because he was driving a rental, there was no garage remote on the visor. He had to activate the door from the wall switch, then quickly slip behind the wheel.

The grinding noise of the door mechanism had him bracing for the attackers to rush the front of the garage. He wasn't disappointed. As the door lifted, the two men he'd seen came pounding around to the front of the house, weapons raised.

He ducked low as the car shot out of the enclosure, bracing for bullets to hit the windshield, but the men were apparently unwilling to risk shots in a residential neighborhood. He barreled down the block and blew through the stop sign, narrowly missing a car that had entered the intersection.

The guy's horn blared after him as he continued down to the next intersection, then took a right and a left, winding through the upscale neighborhood, glancing frequently in the rearview mirror. He'd gotten away, and now he dared to pull to the curb.

"Get in the front."

Francesca exited away from the street and slid into the passenger seat.

The car's seat-belt warning system was now protesting frantically, and he buckled up. She did the same. Before he could start up again, he saw a black sedan coming up behind them fast. With a jerk, he pulled away, executing the same sort of maneuvers that he'd used before, only this time he went down a private drive onto a property that he knew had another entrance around the corner.

It flashed through his mind that he'd been had. What if Francesca had arranged for him to rescue her, and now she'd arranged for these guys to find her again. He scuttled that thought as soon as it had surfaced. She looked like she was in a panic as she twisted around to see behind them.

"How did they find us?"

"I'd like to know. But if they did it so quickly, they can do it again." He kept driving, sometimes taking one of the main avenues and sometimes turning onto cross streets, driving as fast as he dared and looking for some kind of traffic situation that would foul up the guys in the SUV. He saw nothing helpful on the major streets or in the neighborhoods. Switching tactics, he headed for the upscale shopping area along Third Street. Although it was still early, a lot of people were out, both on foot and in cars, probably headed for popular breakfast spots. Glancing in the rearview mirror, he saw that the black car hadn't caught up to them. And ahead, the road was clogged with traffic. More cars were heading for what had turned into a traffic jam. Just before he would have been trapped in the crush, he veered into one of the landscaped parking lots in back of a strip of shops and restaurants. On the street behind him, more cars joined the pileup, blocking the entrance to the lot.

Stopping in a drop-off area, he made sure they were still in the clear before turning to Francesca, "Did your uncle give you anything?" he demanded. "Something you still have with you?"

"Why?"

"The men who showed up at my house knew where to find us, and they've stayed on our tail."

"Then why are we stopping here?"

"Because I bought us a few minutes," *I hope*, he silently added. But he was already plotting two steps ahead.

The panic on her face increased. "He. . . he gave me this." She reached for a gold chain around her neck and pulled out what looked like an antique locket hanging from it."

Zane held out his hand. "Let's see it."

As she lifted the chain over her head, he kept sweeping his gaze through the lot. When she handed him the jewelry, he turned it over and looked at the back. It was flat but with an indentation running all around the edge.

"I think that backing comes off," he told her.

He reached into his pocket for a multipurpose knife. Selecting the screwdriver blade, he handed the pendant back to Francesca, along with the blade. Before the black car could get through the traffic jam and into the parking lot, he drove to the other end and onto the cross street, heading for the water.

Francesca tried to wedge the screwdriver head under the seam at the back of the locket. Instead, it jumped out of the channel and skidded across the surface, scratching the gold.

When she winced, he ordered, "Don't worry about that. Just get it off."

Teeth gritted, she went back to work and was finally able to pry off the backing. There might have been a photo of some long-dead loved one inside. Instead, she pulled out a small round disk which must have been placed there recently.

"What is it?" she asked.

"A tracker."

She caught her breath. "Should I throw it away?"

"No. Hold on to it for a while. I've got a better place to ditch it. And give me back the knife."

She returned the tool as he drove along the street that paralleled the Gulf. Since it wasn't ideal beach weather, he knew more people would be shopping than spreading blankets on the sand, which made a state park along the Gulf an ideal location for his purposes. He turned off at the one he liked best, especially for his nighttime wolf runs along the water. He waved the yearly pass he'd bought at the guard in the gatehouse, then drove through, knowing the bad guys would have to stop and pay a parking fee before following him in.

He had been to this stretch of natural waterfront at night and during the day. There were a lot of parking areas strung out along the road that ran parallel to the Gulf, each separated by several hundred yards of native vegetation. Most guys might not have cared about what grew there, but a werewolf was always interested in the natural surroundings—both the flora and fauna. He headed for a stretch of blacktop that featured a thick screen of sea grape bushes, tall grass, sea oats and beach palms between the parking facilities and the sand. There was also a huge stack of driftwood piled up, probably part of the cleanup after a storm.

As he'd anticipated, there were few people enjoying the park, which fitted in well with his plans—to lead the thugs to the tracker so he could snap their pictures. But he couldn't do it until he knew Francesca was safe.

He pulled into one of the parking areas where a couple of paths led through the vegetation to the beach and pointed in the direction of the water. "Go down there. Hunker down in the underbrush. I'll be back for you as soon as I get rid of them."

Her suddenly panicked face made the breath clog in his throat. She looked like she was afraid he was going to leave her stranded, but he didn't have time to say more than, "Trust me. I'll come back and call. . . honey."

She gave him a tight nod and got out, heading for the greenery bordering the sand. If he could have kept her with him, he would have, but he needed her as far away from the action as he could manage.

Francesca ran toward the Gulf, wondering if they had poison ivy in Florida—or something worse. She found a wide-leafed bush about five feet tall and ducked under the low-hanging branches. Twigs caught in her hair, but once she had scrunched herself into place, she didn't reach to brush them away. As she caught a glimpse of Zane's car heading for the parking lot exit, her stomach clenched. So far she thought he'd been straight with her, but what if he figured she was going to get him killed. What if he was using this opportunity to ditch her?

No, she told herself. He wouldn't do that. Hoping she believed her own assurances, she considered his strategy. He could have thrown the tracker into the mulch of a flower bed at the shopping area. Instead he'd come here. He must have some plan, and she wished he'd had the time to share it with her.

The morning air was chilly, and she shivered, hoping she wasn't making too much noise by shaking the leaves around her —and hoping a snake didn't come slithering toward her through the tall grass.

Her thought about wildlife wasn't too far off the mark. As she peered through her leafy cover, she saw a raccoon waddle out of the vegetation and head toward the nearby picnic area. It looked like it was scavenging for food, but she knew they could carry rabies. She wanted to scare it away, but she couldn't exactly leap up and start shouting and waving her arms. What if she ended in the hospital having to get shots in the stomach to ward off the disease?

Find a burnt hot dog or something, she silently told the animal, *and stay away from me.*

It took her advice, picking up a discarded potato chip bag and reaching inside, scraping up some crumbs before dropping the bag and going in search of better pickings.

The animal's departure left the area in silence except for the sound of the waves sliding against the sand.

She knew her life could depend on staying quiet and calm, but she could feel her heart pounding inside her chest.

Where was Zane? Was he okay, and was he really coming back for her?

———

Zane kept driving toward a hiding place he knew, a small parking area screened by short palms and a low building that must be for maintenance equipment. When he'd hidden the car, he sprinted back the way he'd come, ending up in another parking lot where he tossed the tracker into a trash can that had been stationed in the greenery several dozen yards from the blacktop on the side away from the water. Breathing hard, he had just dived into a clump of low palms when the SUV swung into view.

He holstered his gun, got out his phone, and activated the camera. Soon enough, three burly men clambered out of the black vehicle. They were the same guys who had showed up at the house this morning. One was staring at the screen on his mobile, as he led the others into the underbrush toward the trash can.

Zane snapped their pictures from several angles as they turned to inspect the refuse container.

"What the fuck is this?" one of them asked. "I don't see anybody."

They each took up stations around the can and began tossing

out trash, spreading refuse on the ground as they frantically searched for the piece of jewelry that had led them to this spot.

"Where's the damn locket?" one of them asked.

"Don't see it. It must just be the frigging tracker in here, and we probably already tossed it out."

While they were busy, Zane began moving, staying low as he inched his way to the far side of their vehicle. He kept checking his progress, making sure that the guys were still searching. Finally he reached the car. With the army knife Francesca had returned to him, he slashed the tires on that side of the vehicle.

As he finished, he could still hear them talking around the trash can.

"Okay, so they ditched the tracker, but they gotta be around here. They didn't get that much of a head start."

One of his companions answered with a curse. "Then where did they go?"

"Off into the woods."

As he'd hoped, they started walking along the path through the greenery, heading away from the water, searching for the fugitives.

Staying in the underbrush, Zane backtracked toward his rental. It seemed to take forever to reach it because he was afraid to do anything that would attract their attention. When he finally reached the car, he took a deep breath and slipped behind the wheel. As he started the engine, he looked back, scanning the way he'd come.

The thugs were out of sight, and he pulled out of the parking lot, heading for the previous parking area—where he'd left Francesca. At the spot where he'd left her, he called, "Honey," praying that the toughs weren't going to hear him and come running back. For long moments, nothing happened, and he felt his heart rate accelerate as he called out again.

6

*Z*ane wrapped his hands around the wheel to stop himself from jumping out of the car and starting to beat the bushes looking for Francesca.

Finally he spotted the top of her head as she peeked out from behind a low sea grape tree. When she spotted his car, she dashed along the path and leaped into the passenger seat. As he sped away, he saw movement in the rearview mirror and spotted the bad guys crossing the road, pounding back toward their own transportation. But when they jumped into the car and tried to follow, the heavy vehicle listed to the left, the rims of the tires clunking against the paving.

He saw two of them leap out again and pull their weapons, but he was already too far away with too many trees and bushes in the way for a decent shot.

Zane cut his speed as he headed toward the park exit.

Francesca's teeth were chattering, and he realized he'd sent her down to the windy beach in just her sundress.

"Sorry," he murmured.

"I'm okay," she answered, but he knew it was a lie.

"They can't follow us now," he said as he pulled onto a side street. "They've got to change two tires before they get on the road again."

"That's good, but I thought you were going to get us both killed," she gasped out.

"It was a calculated risk, and it paid off." he shot back as he put a mile between himself and the park before pulling under the shade of a frangipani tree that was next to an open field.

Now that Francesca was in the car, he should keep his hands firmly on the wheel. But he was unable to stop himself from reaching for her and pulling her into his arms.

Her skin felt icy as he ran his hands up and down her arms.

"Sorry I scared you."

She pressed her face against his shoulder. "I'd be dead now if it weren't for you."

He knew she had tried to keep her distance. As she lifted her head toward him, he saw gratitude in her eyes and more—the same desire that he'd been trying to hold in check. That look was like a trigger to all the emotions he'd been denying expression.

He heard a soft growl rise in his throat as he lowered his mouth to hers, giving her a moment to pull back if his own need had made him read her incorrectly. When she didn't push him away, he allowed himself the pleasure of exploring her lips, pressing, rubbing, reveling in all the sensations that he'd only imagined until now.

Some part of his mind registered that it wasn't safe to stay here. Another part told him that the bad guys didn't have two spare tires. And if they did, they'd figure he was a lot farther away.

They were still in the car, and he couldn't do everything he wanted. But he felt reckless enough to pull the lever that slid back his seat, then scooped her up and lifted her onto his lap. Her legs were shifted toward the console. But she twisted her upper body so that her wonderful breasts were pressed to his chest when she wound her arms around his neck.

As he kissed her, he stroked his hands up and down her arms, loving the smooth texture of her skin. With his eyes closed, he could imagine she was naked, and all he'd have to do to cup her breasts would be to ease her a little away from his chest and bring his hands inward. His fingers could imagine the tight points of her nipples, but he somehow kept the impulse to touch her like that in check. Still, there were other sensations to enjoy. Her hip was pressed to his erection, and he longed to swing her body fully around so that she was straddling his lap. Again he kept himself from doing it because he knew with her open to him like that, he might lose any sense of caution. And he was damned if the first time he made love to her would be a furtive encounter in the front seat of a car.

For a few more moments, he let himself enjoy the kiss and the pressure of her body against his, knowing it would have to end soon. Finally, when he was afraid he would tumble over the edge of self-control, he forced himself to lift her back into her seat. She made a sound that was part startled and part loss. Her eyes blinked open, and she stared at him in confusion, then abruptly faced forward, flopping against the seat.

Swiping at her hair, she took several deep breaths. "I'm sorry."

"About what?" he asked, hearing the thick quality of his voice. "I'm the one who picked you up and put you on my lap."

"I let you do it. I don't usually act like that with guys I barely know."

"Both of us are off-balance," he answered. Putting the moment in perspective, he added, "It's not every day you escape from killers with a tracking device."

She dragged in a breath and let it out. "Right."

He'd given her an excuse for her behavior—and his—although he knew it was more than that. They were bonding, and there was no way to escape the pull.

Partly to distract himself and partly because he needed some answers, he let loose with some of the thoughts that had been piling up in his mind. "I've got a lot of questions. "Do you think your uncle knew there was a tracker inside the pendant? How did the bad guys know it was there? Was he working with them, and they had a disagreement?"

She shook her head. "Right, a lot of questions, and I can't answer any of them. I haven't seen him since I was a kid. And I was only at his house for about half an hour when those guys came up from the beach." She finished with a question of her own. "Why would he want to put a tracker on me?"

"To lead him to your father?"

She winced. "That would say that he was using me. And he was working with them—and then they, um, decided he was a liability. In the interrogation, I heard, someone mentioned 'the boss.' Maybe someone else ordered him to get to my father."

"Yeah. Maybe they found out he was playing them. Maybe he'd said he was going to turn you over to them,"

"Use me as bait?"

He dragged in a breath and let it out. "It's as likely as anything else."

"I don't know why he would do any of those things."

Zane dragged in a breath and let it out. "Here's another theory. You were coming down there to see if it was okay to take him to your father. What if you decided you didn't like him? You could leave without connecting them—and he'd still be able to trace you back home. But with him dead, we can only guess his motivation. And the remark about 'the boss' had nothing to do with you."

"Can a tracker work over hundreds of miles?"

"Probably not."

"Then what good would it be to find my father."

"He could see where you were flying to—then go there and start the search again. Did he and your dad part on good terms?"

"I don't know that either. I was just a little girl. And if he went into witness protection, maybe they didn't have any way to communicate before he went into hiding."

Zane nodded, wondering how that fed into the whole picture.

She looked around at the street and the field that stretched away from the curb. "They may not be able to zero in on us anymore, but we can't stay here. Where are we going?"

"Hopefully, the last place in Naples they would look for us." He pulled away from the roadside and drove to a discount department store on the outskirts of town. As he swung into a parking spot, she asked, "What are we doing here?"

"We both look like we've been crawling around hunting for alligator eggs. We're going to need to look a little more respectable before our next stop."

"But I don't have any money or any credit cards."

"I told you not to worry about that. Just pick up three or four everyday outfits."

He was too worried to let her out of his sight for long. Inside the store he followed her through the women's department as she picked out some nice-looking tee shirts and those cut-off pants he didn't know the name for. When she'd put together several outfits and added some underwear to the cart, he waited while she changed clothes, then had her follow him to the men's department where he bought slacks and a couple of tees. He changed quickly, relieved that she was standing by their cart when he came out of the dressing room.

"That suits you," she said.

"You too. Good choices. Let's get some toothpaste and a few

other things we might need." He gave her a critical look. "Like a hairbrush. And we can make a stop at the restrooms to wash up."

She wrinkled her face. "Thanks." Another thought struck her. "I don't have a purse. Maybe I'd better pick up a cheap one."

"Yeah. You'd stand out without one."

On the way to the drugstore section, he also bought a medium-sized suitcase.

After they'd cleaned up, he paid for their purchases in cash and was watchful as they returned to his car. So far, so good. He wished he could get some different license plates, but that would represent another kind of risk. And the car wasn't going to be out where the thugs could stumble over it.

"Now what?" she asked.

"The perfect hiding place."

She gave him a questioning look, but he stayed silent and headed for a strip of highway lined with tall buildings separated by tracts of manicured greenery. He turned in at a driveway that led to a large beige-colored building with towers at the corners.

Before reaching the building, he stopped along the driveway and stowed his gun in the suitcase. This wasn't the kind of establishment where you came in with a weapon, and if he thought this place was safe, he'd better act like it.

Pulling into the drive again, he headed for the entrance. They passed a three-tiered circular fountain and pulled up under a porte cochere.

As soon as the car stopped, a young man in navy blue Bermudas and a white shirt came running over. "Checking in, sir?"

"Yes."

"We'll take care of the car for you." The attendant gestured, "Leave it over there."

"Where are we?" Francesca whispered as Zane came around to her side of the vehicle.

"The Ritz-Carlton."

She gave him a shocked look. "Isn't that expensive?"

"Yeah. It's the top hotel in Naples." When they were out of earshot, he added. "I figure this is the last place anyone is going to look for us."

He got the luggage from the back seat and led her inside where he turned to the left past a round marble-topped table with a huge flower arrangement in the middle. A little farther on was a long marble counter where they waited for one of the clerks to free up.

When an attractive blond motioned them over, Zane stepped to the counter. "We'd like a room for the night," he said. "On a low floor. My wife doesn't like heights."

"Certainly. Credit card."

He handed over a card, and the desk clerk ran it through the machine.

"I'll get a bellperson to help you with your luggage," she said.

"I can handle it. Can you give the parking attendant our room number?"

"Certainly, Mr. Montgomery. The elevators are to your right."

"Thanks."

Francesca's head jerked toward him, and he took her hand, squeezing.

She pressed her lips together as they headed down a wood-paneled hallway toward the elevator. When they reached the third floor, he checked the signs, then turned left.

"What does it cost to stay here?" she asked.

"Don't worry about it. I put it on my expense account."

"You can do that?"

"In this case, yes."

As they walked toward the room, he kept thinking—now what? He'd cleverly arranged for them to be alone together in luxury accommodations.

After locking the door behind them, he surveyed the room.

It was elegant but decorated in very neutral colors. And there were two double beds, which was good. That made it look less like he'd brought her to . . .

Without finishing the thought, he set down the suitcase and crossed to the window. The room had a balcony, with another below it. Probably he could use that escape route if he had to. Would Francesca be up to climbing down? They had a partial Gulf view, with another set of rooms to their right and others facing them in a farther wing of the hotel.

He shifted his gaze to the blue water, which was separated from the hotel by what appeared to be a swamp crossed by a couple of boardwalks. At the far edge was a wooden building that could have been an old-time seafood restaurant. Probably it looked charming up close.

Behind him Francesca cleared her throat. "You probably think I fall into the arms of every guy . . ."

"Who rescues you from contract killers?"

"Is that what they are?"

He turned to face her. "Well, killers. Maybe mob hit men."

"You're trying to defuse the situation between us now that we're locked up together in a bedroom."

"Yeah, and trying to be realistic." She was taking this conversation in a direction that was dangerous. If he could put some physical distance between them, he would, but there was a graver danger in leaving her alone.

He laid the suitcase on a luggage stand, pulled out his laptop, and walked to the desk across from the beds.

"I have to get some information."

"How?"

"I'm starting with my office. They may have something for me."

She gave him a long look. "I'll let you work."

"Yeah, thanks."

She turned away and reached for the TV remote. He heard

her turn on the set as he booted up the computer. When he gave her a quick glance, she had kicked off her sandals and piled up the pillows on one of the beds.

Thank God she was going to ignore him for the moment, he thought as he waited for his e-mail to come up.

7

Zane found a message from Frank Decorah, authorizing him to do what he already had done. Although he'd expected it, he couldn't hold back his feeling of relief as he composed an answer, starting with an update on what had happened since their last communication. He'd initially thought the safest place for Francesca was Decorah headquarters. Now he told Frank they needed to stay in the area to get more information. But he also wanted some help from headquarters. After describing what had gone down this morning, he said,

"The uncle's name was Angelo Lucci. The father went into the witness protection program about twenty years ago as Glen Turner. Presumably his last name was also Lucci. And Francesca thinks he was mob connected. I'll check up on Angelo from this end and also on the Web." He finished by switching to his phone and sending the pictures he'd snapped of the men who had come after him and Francesca. "These are the guys who tried to kill us. If you can get a line on any of them, I'd appreciate it."

After checking his other mail, he prowled around the Internet looking for anything else that might be helpful. Apparently Angelo Lucci had kept a low profile after arriving in Naples. Property records told Zane that Lucci had moved to his current home fifteen years ago, but there was nothing else about him online until his house had burned down the night before. As far as the authorities knew, he was missing. Which meant they hadn't found a body in the ashes of the house. But Francesca had heard the men talking about disposing of the body. What had they done with the uncle—weighted him down with rocks and left him in the water somewhere? Or had they used a bone saw to dismember him—Saudi Arabia style.

The grisly thought made him glance up at Francesca. Apparently she hadn't read his thoughts because she was still pretending to be absorbed by whatever was on the TV.

He swivelled toward the window, noting that the sun was low in the sky. He'd managed to spend a lot of time avoiding the woman a few yards away. When he swung toward the bed where she was camping out, he found her looking at him.

"Are we going to stay in this room ignoring each other for the rest of the evening? Or can we go downstairs and have something to eat?"

He considered the request. They'd been cooped up in a confined space for hours together, and ordering room service was only going to prolong the togetherness. But he'd chosen this hotel because nobody was likely to wander in off the street, and the kind of guys who had showed up at his rental in the morning would stand out here like a dogcatcher at a fancy dress ball.

"There are a couple of restaurants downstairs. We're probably dressed well enough for the more moderate one."

She might have come back with some kind of snappy remark. Instead she just shrugged and said, "Okay."

The restaurant was along a covered walkway that looked out toward the pool. Since it was early, they had no trouble getting a seat at a table for two.

"Can I have a drink?" Francesca asked.

He considered the question. "You can. I'd better not."

"Then I'll just have iced tea."

When the waiter came, she asked for the tea. Zane stuck with water. For dinner she ordered a seafood risotto. He got an expensive dry-aged-beef burger and fries.

Despite his assessment that having a meal outside their room was safe, he kept scanning the dining room but didn't see anyone who looked like a threat.

They sat in silence for a few minutes. Finally, he asked, "You like Italian food?"

"My mom liked to cook it. Luckily, Italian is a fairly standard American ethnic cuisine. Nobody thought it weird that Mrs. Lisa Turner made it a specialty."

"Uh huh."

"And you're a burger kind of guy?"

He shrugged. "It seems easiest."

Again, the conversation lapsed. He heard her drag in a breath and let it out before saying, "In the car we reached for each other. Now you're working to keep your distance."

He answered with a tight nod.

"Why do I feel so drawn to you?"

The blatant question was the crux of the issue between them, and just her asking it made his skin feel hot and cold at the same time.

He should keep his mouth shut, but he heard himself saying, "A genetic trait in my family."

"Oh come on. What's that supposed to mean? You give off some kind of pheromones that attract Italian women?"

Now what was he going to say? That when a werewolf met his life mate, there was no escaping the relationship? Right, she'd love to hear that she's fallen into the arms of a wolf.

He was saved from answering by the arrival of the food. When the waiter had left she said, "Well?"

Automatically, he took a bite of the burger and chewed. The

meat was a lot more done than he liked, and he wanted to throw away the bread, but he chewed and swallowed before saying, "The men in my family click with a certain kind of woman?"

"What kind? Loose women?"

Was he really having this conversation in a restaurant? Maybe it was safer than in their room.

"I didn't actually mean a type. I mean, when we meet the woman who's right for us—we bond." Just saying it made his throat constrict and his heart start to thump.

The silence stretched between them as she focused on her risotto for a few moments.

Finally she said, "Are you talking about some kind of mystic connection?"

"I guess I am."

He didn't know how he had expected this conversation to go, but when she made a dismissive sound, his reaction was sharp. "When we kissed—you didn't feel like lightning struck you?"

"No," she shot back, her expression defiant.

"You're lying."

8

Z ane saw Francesca look around the restaurant to make sure
nobody was close enough to be listening before she said,
"You say we've bonded—so you can take my emotional tempera-
ture just like that."

He hadn't intended to get into any of this. But the words and
the sarcasm in her voice were too much for him.

Their eyes locked. If they'd been alone, he would have
crossed the space between them and folded her into his arms to
prove his point. But not in a public dining room. Still, his gaze
burned into her, and he saw her flush, then lower her head and
go back to her food.

Neither of them said much as they finished their meals.

"Do we have to go right back to the room?" she asked when
they stepped outside. "Or can we enjoy this fancy place a little
bit?"

He'd like to take her back there for safekeeping, instead he
let her lead him on a stroll around the manicured grounds, then
across the boardwalk that led to the Gulf.

He couldn't call the walk companionable. As they stepped

onto the sand, tension radiated between them, and he wondered if it was going to flair out of control. He pictured himself dragging her into the sand dunes for some intimate body contact.

Instead he clenched his teeth and turned back toward the hotel.

When he'd closed the door of the room, she gave him a long look, which was like a spark hitting dry tinder. For a long moment, neither of them moved.

"Have it your way," she murmured as she turned on the television again—to a channel which seemed to be focused on home remodeling.

With a deep sigh, he booted his computer. He'd put himself in this situation, and it was his own damn fault. What would be wrong with showing her what the two of them were going to mean to each other? The images of naked bodies entwined on the bed flashing in his mind were very tempting. But his duty was to keep her safe, not give in to his wolf nature.

When he opened his mail, he found an interim report from Teddy Granada at Decorah saying that he hadn't yet gotten anything on the father. But there was an arrest record for the uncle. He'd been brought up on money laundering charges, but a skilled lawyer had gotten him off.

Sometime during the evening, Francesca went into the bathroom, took off her pants and got under the covers wearing her tee shirt and panties. He hung the "Do Not Disturb" sign on the outside of the door and slipped into his own bed, similarly dressed.

He told himself the best thing was to get some rest, and to his surprise, he drifted off pretty quickly.

A noise woke him sometime in the night, and he was immediately on alert, reaching for the gun that he'd wedged under the pillow on the other side of his bed.

With the Sig in hand, he lay in the dark, listening for more sounds—like the doorknob turning, or footsteps crossing the room. But he heard nothing—besides a muffled sob coming from Francesca's bed.

He whipped toward her, softly calling her name. She didn't respond, and he didn't know if she was caught in a dream or if she was deliberately not answering him.

He waited for several moments. When he heard her moan, he figured it was the former.

Easing out of his own bed, he laid the gun on the nightstand and crossed the space between the two beds. His eyes had adjusted to the dim light, and now he could see her thrashing around as she moaned and called out, "Help me. Please help me."

The sight of her in distress tore at him,

He called her name again, and when she didn't answer, he slid onto the side of the bed, cupping her shoulder. She woke instantly, her body jerking and her arm striking out at him, and he had to catch her hand to keep from being hit again.

"Francesca, it's me, Zane. You were having a nightmare."

Her head came up, and she looked up at him in confusion. "Zane?"

"Yes. Are you okay?"

Her voice shook as she said, "No."

He heard the gritty quality of his own voice as he asked, "What was the dream?"

"I need you to hold me."

Not a good idea, he thought. But what he had told her downstairs was true. They had bonded, and the anguish in her voice wrenched at his heart and he couldn't stop himself from pulling aside the covers and slipping into bed with her.

She was trembling, and her skin was icy. He pulled her into the warmth of his body and stroked his hand over her back and shoulders and into her hair. Neither one of them was wearing much, and he was all too conscious of his bare legs tangling with hers.

By small degrees, she stopped trembling.

"Better?"

"A little."

"What was the dream?" he asked again.

She swallowed hard. "It was the same stuff that happened yesterday. A lot of it was pretty realistic. I was back in Uncle Angelo's house. I was hiding in the closet, listening to the men beating him up. Then I heard them running around the house, opening and closing drawers and cabinets, shouting my name. They went quiet, and then the fire started. I got out of the house and I ran toward the fence. The gate was open, and I saw the big dog down the beach. Yesterday he saved me from the men. In the dream he was different. I called out to him begging him to help me. In real life he did. In the dream he just stood there, staring at the men as they grabbed me and dragged me off."

That was too much for Zane.

"He's a wolf. The wolf would never do that."

"A wolf? How do you know?"

He silently cursed himself for saying that. Now he was stuck with making something up. "I saw him. Your mind just made up his reaction because it was a nightmare, and you were scared." That could be the truth, but was it more? Was she unconsciously reacting to his putting distance between them all day?

"It was pretty real."

"I'm so sorry." He ached to tell her that he was the wolf, and he would never let anything happen to her. But he couldn't say that. And he couldn't say that maybe the dream was his fault.

Now the frustration of keeping silent was too much to bear.

All he could do was show her the wolf's true feelings. Without giving himself time to think about it any longer, he lowered his mouth to hers. He had intended the kiss to be gently and reassuring. Instead it was searing, a kiss that said all the things he couldn't say out loud. There was a dark moment when he thought she didn't feel the same things he did. Was he wrong about the two of them?

No. He felt her response, and his uncertainty evaporated like mist burned away by the Florida sun.

Thank God.

He slanted his lips over hers, angled his head, took her mouth in every way that he could, and when his tongue demanded entrance, she opened for him.

Heat leaped inside him as he breached that barrier, reveling in the joy of tasting her.

He wanted her to know what they meant to each other—what they would mean to each other.

His hands slid down her body cupping her bottom so that he could pull her against his aching cock. He wanted her the way he had never wanted another woman. But pushing her into intimacy would be the biggest mistake of his life. Going any farther had to be her choice.

When he finally lifted his head, the dazed expression in her eyes made his chest tighten. Probably he looked similarly gobsmacked. He had gotten into her bed to comfort her. He was feeling far from comfortable.

He told himself he should stand up. Probably he should go into the bathroom and stick his head under a freezing shower. If you could get freezing water in Florida.

"I didn't mean for that to happen."

"But it did."

She swallowed hard, and her voice softened. "I know. The weird thing is that I trust you. I'm not so sure about myself." She paused, then murmured, "I guess there's only one way to find out."

As she came back into his arms, relief was like a spring thunderstorm pounding through him. He was frozen in place, and when he didn't move, she lifted her face to his.

A few minutes ago, he had kissed her with desperation. It

had been the desperation of the wolf afraid he would lose his mate. Now he wanted her to know how good—how right—it could be between them.

He kissed her softly, tenderly, forcing nothing, letting her silently take the lead.

As their lips explored, her hands stroked restlessly over his back as though she wanted to memorize his contours. Eyes closed, he did the same, simply absorbing the feel of her.

Once again he silently acknowledged that he needed her more than he had ever needed anyone in his life. And he sensed that she needed him with the same intensity because what they could give each other had become as necessary as breathing.

He lifted his head, but only a fraction as his lips played with hers, thankful that he had brought her to this nicely appointed room and not some cheap motel off the highway.

Francesca nestled in his arms. He had said they were bonded. Just that simple thought sent prickles of anticipation shimmering across his skin.

"Turn on the light," she murmured. "I want to see you. I want to see all of you."

He reached for the lamp on the table beside the bed. The flare of brightness made her blink but only for a moment. When she opened her eyes again, she saw he was watching her with the intensity of a wolf that had cornered his prey.

The wolf? Why did she keep coming back to that feral animal?

She should be afraid, but she kept her gaze fixed on him as she sat up, reached for the hem of her tee shirt, and pulled it over her head.

The plain white bra she'd bought this morning wasn't exactly fuck-me underwear, but the intimacy of revealing so much made her breath catch.

"I thought you might be shy with me," he said, his tone gritty.

"I thought I might be, too. But I can't muster any inhibitions." She tried to sound bold, but she could hear the hint of a quaver in her voice.

"Are you sure about this?"

"Yes," she answered when she knew it might be a lie.

He sat up so that he could strip off his own tee shirt. She loved his broad chest. She hadn't thought chest hair was exciting. It was on him.

Reaching out, she stroked her lips against his shoulder and ran her fingers through that crisp dark chest hair, gratified that his breath caught. It caught again when she glided her fingertips across his nipples.

Pulling her close, he reached for the clasp at the back of her bra and unhooked it. When he'd slipped the straps off her shoulders and tossed the garment to join the others on the floor, she could barely breathe.

"Lord, you are gorgeous," he murmured before lifting her breasts in his hands. She felt the tips go diamond hard from his touch. As he bent to suck one into his mouth, she cupped her hands around the back of his head.

"That's so good," she murmured.

He lifted his mouth away for a moment so he could say, "On this end, too."

She laughed, and he did also, telling her that they were on the same wavelength.

He went back to his delicious attentions, and she arched into the caress, feeling the passion flaring between them.

She kept her gaze on him as she tugged off her panties. Just removing that last bit of clothing made heat gather in her secret, feminine core.

Her gaze locked to his, and she said, "I want you naked, too."

"Oh yeah," he answered, doing as she asked.

He was in her bed, naked and aroused, and she drank her fill of his magnificent body. Heat rose in his face, but he stayed where he was, letting her feast her gaze on him.

"You are like a Greek statue," she murmured. "Well, except for one thing. I never saw an ancient statue with a hard-on."

They both laughed again. As the tension broke, he rolled to his side and gathered her to him.

The feel of his skin against hers was glorious. She pressed against him for long moments before drawing back as his hand slipped between them, playing over her breasts. He stroked them, reshaped them to his touch, and then drew small and smaller circles around her nipples, until his fingers slid against the sides of those hardened tips.

She gasped at his knowing touch, then gasped again as his thumbs and fingers closed around the throbbing points of pleasure.

"Oh."

One of his hands traveled lower, finding all the sensitive places that were responding so willingly to his touch.

She felt herself tremble as his fingers slid over her belly, tangled in the curly hair at the juncture of her legs, then slipped lower into the warm folds of her feminine flesh.

She lifted her hips, wordlessly telling him that she wanted more.

He raised up on one elbow, his hot gaze burning into hers.

"Please, don't make me wait."

But he did make her wait while he pushed her higher and higher until she knew she was almost at the breaking point.

He knew it too, because he covered her body with his. When his cock filled her, she was lost to everything but the wonder of the moment.

She took him deeply into herself, embracing the knowledge that their joining was so much more than physical pleasure.

When he stilled, her fingers dug into his buttocks. "Please."

He looked down at her for a long moment as though committing this joining to memory. Then he began to move, and she knew he was trying to keep his movements slow. She clung to him, raising her hips, following his rhythm as she felt small tremors shake her. They built to earthquake proportions, exploding through her in a shower of pleasure. Her climax sent his hips pumping, and moments later she heard his shout of satisfaction.

They were both slick with sweat when he rolled to his side, kissing her, keeping his arms around her. She snuggled against him, marveling at how content, how complete she felt.

―――――――

Zane didn't have to ask, "Was it good for you?"

He knew it was because of the way she cuddled into him, limp and satisfied.

He wanted to turn off his brain and sink into sleep holding her in his arms. But too many thoughts were vying for attention in his mind.

They were on the run from professional killers, and he had let his guard slip. If the men who had been after them had come through the door a few moments ago, he wouldn't have been able to do much about it.

He cursed himself, and she must have sensed his change of mood.

"What?"

"I rushed you into making love, and I should be trying to figure out why you're in danger."

She gave him an indignant look. "You didn't rush me into

anything. I made it damn near impossible for you to do anything else."

"Why?"

She kept her gaze on him. "You said we had bonded. I wanted to know if it was true."

"Was it?"

"Yes." She looked away. "And that kind of scares me."

"Yeah."

"It scares you, too?"

"Yes, because it's only going to happen to me once."

Her breath caught.

"And that means guarding you has become the most important thing in the world. Now I know I need to keep my head screwed on straight." He clenched his hands at his sides. "I wasn't acting much like a bodyguard just now."

"I pushed you."

"I let myself be pushed. It won't happen again."

She made a small sound that tore at him. "Let's hope that's not true. It would be a shame to be bonded with a man who was only going to make love to me once."

"You know what I mean. I want you out of danger first."

There were a lot more things he wanted to say, but he knew he couldn't. Maybe if he told her she'd just made love with a werewolf that would change her perspective. But he wasn't willing to risk revealing that piece of information. What if he told her, and he lost her?

9

Z ane climbed out of her bed and went back to his own. He didn't turn his head, but he felt her staring at him. Closing his eyes, he tried to get back to sleep, but that was impossible.

When light seeped in at the edge of the blackout curtain, he got up.

Seeing her looking at him, he said, " I need to check my mail." It was true but it was also a way to cut off personal conversation.

"Sure. I'll get dressed."

She got up, opened the suitcase and took out some clothes, then disappeared into the bathroom. As he heard the water running in the shower, he pictured her naked and stepping under the water. When he started getting turned on again, he ruthlessly switched his attention to his e-mail and found a communication from Teddy Granada at Decorah.

Using FBI and local law enforcement databases, Teddy had been able to identify one of the men in the pictures. He was Conrad Tuckerman, called Connie for short, and he'd been in and out of trouble with the law for years. He was suspected of a couple of murders although there had never been enough evidence to arrest him. He was also known to hang out at a local bar in town called the Tin Man, which took its name from a nearby shopping mall called Tin City. The buildings of the rambling downscale mall were all made of corrugated tin.

Zane figured his best bet was to check out the bar, but first he wanted to switch cars, since Tuckerman and his friends were very familiar with his current rental.

Francesca came out of the bathroom, dressed in her short pants and another tee shirt they'd bought the day before.

"I'll get ready, and we can go to breakfast," he said.

She nodded, and he noted from her expression that she seemed to be back in the mode where she was pretending they were just friends sharing this room. Well, that's what he'd said he wanted. Still, he couldn't help feeling the sting of her indifference.

As he gathered up his own clothes and stepped into the bathroom, he wished he'd talked to his brother or some of his cousins about how they'd handled things when they'd bonded with their mates.

But that wasn't something that werewolves talked about. In the wild, a wolf pack was led by an alpha male and all the other wolves were subservient to him. It was different with werewolves, who had all descended from one man who had begged the ancient gods for powers beyond the human. In getting his wish, he'd acquired the ability to shape-shift, and his male descendants carried a gene for lycanthropy.

But unlike with wolves in the wild, shape-shifters were all alpha males, each one the leader of his own pack. Before he bonded, it was a pack of one. When he had a wife and family, they were the members of his pack. Zane knew that in generations past, the alpha werewolf lorded it over his family. Modern guys were more enlightened. Also, not so long ago, the alpha males didn't get along with each other. But in this case, Frank

Decorah had helped them learn how to work together—although there were still challenges when one wolf thought another had stepped over the line.

This history meant that the Marshall men didn't share a lot of personal information with each other. He'd seen a transformation in his brother, Knox, when he'd come home from Western Maryland with a mate. But Zane had sensed his brother didn't want to talk about the bonding process, partly because some very bad guys had put him into a drugged stupor before he'd met Maggie. And Zane wasn't going to call him up now for advice. That wasn't the way of the alpha male.

He finished showering and dressing and came out of the bathroom. For a moment of panic, he didn't see Francesca in the room. Then he realized that she was on the balcony, leaning on the railing and staring out at the Gulf. There were other hotel guests also enjoying the Florida morning, and his first thought was to rush outside and herd her back inside. But he curtailed the impulse. Instead he opened the sliding glass door and asked,

"Ready for some breakfast."

"I guess." She stepped back into the room and closed the door behind her.

"I want to make a stop on the way."

"Where?"

"There's a car rental office off the hallway that leads to the restaurant. If I get a different car, the bad guys will have less chance of spotting us driving around town."

"Are we driving around town?"

He cursed himself for having voiced part of his plans. "I have a lead on one of the men who showed up at my rental yesterday. I need to check it out."

"Not by yourself."

He gave her a hard look. "I'm not putting you at risk again—not when you're safe here."

"You don't have a choice, because you're not going to leave

me hiding in a posh hotel while you go out and do your detective work."

He struggled not to clench his teeth. He should have kept his mouth shut, but there was no point in arguing with her now.

After he'd reserved a car, they headed for the dining room where the woman at the hostess station greeted them like old friends. And as they took a table against a wall, he saw a fair number of the same faces as the night before.

He didn't like it. And he didn't like that the woman who'd given them their menus was now talking to the hostess. They both glanced in his and Francesca's direction then quickly away when they saw he'd noticed the attention.

Shit. What was that about? Were they speculating on their marital status or what? The Ritz-Carlton might be an upscale little enclave at the water's edge in Naples, but anyone could mention the couple they had seen there. That might have been a paranoid thought, but he wasn't going to dismiss paranoia when it might keep Francesca alive.

Traditional breakfast food had never been a favorite of Zane's. He ordered steak and eggs and left most of the food on his plate, while Francesca packed away an order of fruit and pancakes.

They spoke little during the meal and were in and out of the restaurant and back in their room in under forty minutes, partly because he was constantly scanning the dining room instead of talking to her.

As soon as the bedroom door closed behind them, she whirled toward him. "Why were you watching everybody down there?"

"Because some of them noticed us."

"I thought you said this place was safe."

"I thought so. Now I think we're too conspicuous. I think it's better if we move somewhere more private."

She folded her arms across her middle as he pulled out his phone and got Teddy at Decorah.

"I'd like some help with rental properties," he told the Decorah IT guy.

"Not exactly my specialty."

"But it's better if I don't leave a trail of requests for information around the Internet."

"Right."

"I don't suppose you can find me a cabin in a swamp."

"Doubtful."

"Well, if we can't disappear into the wilderness, can you give me a line on houseboat and cabin cruiser rentals in the area, in marinas that are off the beaten track?"

"Let me send the listings to our Dropbox. That way nobody can see it but Decorah personnel."

"Good idea. And include the specs on the marinas."

Zane booted his laptop and waited for a Dropbox entry with pictures of the crafts available at various marinas.

The first one came through in about twenty minutes with a notation that more would follow.

After looking at pictures of boats and taking a couple of virtual tours, he had Teddy do the booking.

When he finished, he looked up to find Francesca watching him.

"Are you going to let me in on your deliberations?" she inquired.

"You probably gathered from my end of the conversation that I want to move us to a boat."

"If you're worried about people seeing us around the hotel, we could hang a "Do Not Disturb" sign on the door and stay in here making love."

Her words sent a very enticing picture leaping into his mind —the two of them in the closest bed, her body under his—but he wasn't going to take the bait.

They stared at each other across six feet of charged space. He wanted to respond to the challenge she'd tossed him. But last night had been a slip in judgment on his part, and it wasn't going to happen again until he knew killers weren't coming after her.

He wouldn't let himself turn away. Instead he forced himself to keep facing her as he took a few moments to get his hormones under control. Finally he said, "We've rented a cabin cruiser in an out-of-the-way marina where we won't be seeing a lot of people. If we're lucky, the mobsters will think we cleared out of town."

"And went where?"

"Back north."

"How did we get away? Don't you think they're watching the airports and the car rental companies?"

"We could have headed right out of town."

The conversation was interrupted when Zane got a call that the new rental car had arrived.

"Our ride's here. You stay put until we're ready to roll."

10

Zane grabbed their suitcase and his equipment case and stepped into the hall where he put the "Do Not Disturb" sign on the door. Once it closed behind him, he took several deep breaths. If you'd asked him what kind of mate he wanted, he would have chosen a woman who didn't challenge every damn decision he made. In the next moment, he shook his head, silently admitting that he'd be lying to himself. He liked Francesca's assertiveness. He'd like it better if he didn't worry it was going to get her killed.

On the ground floor, he signed the contract for the new rental, a silver Chevy that looked nothing like their previous ride.

Once he'd finished the transactions, he called Francesca on the house phone and asked her to meet him at the registration desk.

"I'm sorry you could only spend one night with us," the pretty blond clerk said.

"Yes. Next time we'll stay longer." He turned to Francesca. "Won't we dear?"

"I hope so," she answered, keeping up the happily married couple act.

Once in the Chevy, they headed south, toward Marco Island, with Zane looking frequently in the rearview mirror to make sure they weren't being followed.

"Have you ever lived on a boat?" he asked, as they turned onto the coast road, then took Route 41 south.

"No, have you?"

"Once, when we were staking out some guys who were smuggling drugs into the country. They were coming in to a particular marina, and I rented a boat near their slip so I could watch their comings and goings."

"Why weren't the cops handling the operation?" she asked.

"Because the owner of the marina had been in trouble with the law earlier, and he didn't want the authorities involved. Plus he didn't want to be blamed for the smuggling operation. He just wanted the lowlifes out of there."

"They'd just set up shop somewhere else."

"Yeah, but we agreed to keep tabs on where they were going and turn the case over to the local PD once our marina guy was out of the picture."

"Clever."

He debated telling her more stories that would keep her mind off their current circumstances. Instead, he decided it was better to get as much information from her as he could.

"Have you told me everything you know about your uncle?" he asked.

Francesca stifled the feeling that she was about to be interrogated. She had told him what she knew. Now she struggled to keep Zane's question from ruffling her.

"Like I said, I don't know much. I never did know much. He

was just my dad's brother who used to get together with us on holidays."

"You only saw him at Christmas and Easter?"

"That was just a kind of shorthand answer. He was around at other times."

"For meals, or did he have business with your dad?"

"Maybe for business. When he came over, my mother would invite him to eat with us. When we cut off all communication with the people we'd known, he disappeared from our lives like everyone else."

"Was he married?" Zane asked.

That stopped her. "Good question. He used to bring a woman he called Aunt Marjory with him, sometimes. I don't know if they were married or what happened to her."

"I'd like to get a line on her. I suppose her name's not Marjory Lucci, although it could be."

"She might not have been his wife, but she was defiantly— intimate with him."

His head snapped toward her. "You were eight. How did you know?"

"She used to kiss him and sit on his lap."

He laughed. "I guess that's pretty up-front."

She shot Zane a sidewise look. "Or maybe she was staking a claim on him. Either way, my mom didn't approve of public displays of affection."

He was quiet for a while, probably trying to decide if there was some way to find out about the mistress.

"What town did you live in before you joined the program?" he asked.

"Morristown, New Jersey."

"We should see if there's any record of your uncle there. Or nearby."

"It would be old."

"Yeah, he's been in Florida for at least fifteen years."

"How do you know?"

"Tax records."

When Zane was quiet again for several minutes, she asked, "Where are we going—exactly?"

"There's a lot of recreational boating down here—with a ton of marinas on the rivers that flow into the Gulf. I figure we shouldn't pick the classiest place. We're going to Cypress Creek. It's not a dump, but it's below average in big-ticket amenities. No pool or gym, for example, and no playground."

She hadn't thought about the Florida boating culture. "They have stuff like that at a marina?"

"Apparently. Some even have pool tables and upscale restaurants. Cypress Creek is smaller. It's not a place where we're going to have a lot of neighbors."

"But they do have short-term boat rentals?"

"We're renting from a private owner. He makes his boat, the Lady Slipper, available to vacationers when he's not in the area."

They arrived at the property about twenty minutes later, and she watched Zane carefully checking the surroundings, impressed with his attention to detail. Really, she should stop protesting his precaution. Of course, if she did that, she'd have to admit she was still in imminent danger.

She shuddered.

"What?"

"I just flashed back on the car chase yesterday," she conceded.

He unbuckled his seat belt, pulled her to him, and cradled her in his arms. "We'll get through this."

It was tempting to let the moment stretch. Feeling his arms around her had given her a sense of security from that first time on the beach. Instead, she straightened and studied the marina. It looked to have around thirty slips with about two-thirds of them occupied.

Shifting away from the water, she saw well-kept tropical

plantings around the office, not as luxurious as what her uncle had, but nice.

Next door to the office was a Laundromat and a convenience store. It looked like an okay place, but she caught a doubtful expression on Zane's face.

"What?"

"When I checked out pictures of this outfit. I expected fewer boats—fewer people."

"Is that a problem?"

"I hope not." He sighed. "But it's probably better if you're seen as little as possible. Why don't you wait in the car while I register?"

"Okay."

As Zane headed for the office, she slouched down in her seat. When he came back, he was holding the rental agreement and a list of rules.

"The Lady Slipper is down there." He pointed to a short wooden dock where several boats were moored.

After grabbing their luggage from the trunk, Zane led her toward their craft. Although she didn't know a lot about boats, she could see that this one was a classic design, maybe twenty or thirty years old, but it seemed to be well maintained, with fresh varnish on the exposed wood.

"There's a smaller boat on the back," she commented as they inspected their new home.

"Yes, a dinghy, on the swim platform."

"Give me a moment." He switched on the power connection to the marina's system then helped her onto the back deck where there was bench seating along the rails and a couple of patio chairs. The surface swayed slightly as their weight tipped the craft to the side.

She stood for a moment, trying to get used to the gentle swaying before stepping into the main cabin.

Apparently the small space functioned as a living room,

dining room, galley combination. The couches and eating area were all built in. The upholstery was faded but clean. After giving the seating section a quick inspection, she crossed to the galley, taking note of the small fridge and the two-burner stove, which she assumed ran on propane. Next she checked for pots and pans, utensils and finally provisions.

"The cooking equipment's okay, but there's almost nothing here to eat, unless you're into peanut butter and jelly."

He wrinkled his nose.

Taking in his reaction, she said, "We'll have to get supplies."

"Or I can bring in burgers."

She countered with, "We passed a small shopping center a little way down the road. We can get groceries."

After inspecting the common areas, they descended to a lower level with two small cabins, on either side of the hall, each with a curtain instead of a door. Pulling aside one curtain, she stared at a bunk with storage drawers underneath and a shelf above with a little railing along the edge to prevent things from falling off when the boat was moving.

"Which room do you want?" Zane asked.

She gave him a considering look. "If I need to have my own room, you pick one, I'll take the other," she answered, knowing she sounded surly.

"I'm trying to keep you safe," he snapped.

She felt things going downhill again as she asked, "How does keeping your distance make me safe?"

"It focuses my attention where it should be."

She dragged in a breath and let it out. "Have it your way."

"Do you think I don't want to make love to you right now?" he shot back.

"Do you?" She lowered her gaze to the front of his pants.

She could see with that look, she might as well have closed her hand around his cock. Keeping his palms at his sides, he said, "You know damn well I do. But first, I want to be sure the men

74

who killed your uncle don't kill you. Do you want to be making love a couple of seconds before you get shot?"

The comment landed like a thud against her chest, and she staggered back.

Seeing her reaction, he closed the space between them and pulled her against himself. As they stood swaying in the narrow passageway, he murmured, "I'm sorry. I think we're both on edge."

"Uh huh." Lowering her head to his shoulder, she held on to him, hating to feel needy, but at the same time thankful for his embrace. It flashed through her mind that she could push him now, literally push him against the paneled wall and plaster herself to him. But she wasn't going to pull any tricks.

"I know you're trying to do your job," she whispered.

"If it were just a job, it would be a lot easier."

"Yes. It's frustrating to hear you've 'bonded' with a guy but have to keep your distance."

"You know I feel the same way. Just think how good it's going to be when we make love again."

The words were like a jolt of arousal, but she kept it under control."

They clung together in the companionway, swaying slightly as the craft caught the wake from a speedboat coming in to dock.

Telling herself she was being stupid to keep testing his resolve, Francesca pushed away and headed back upstairs to the main room. Opening the fridge, she was glad to find bottles of water. When she heard Zane behind her, she opened a bottle for each of them, and they took a seat at the dining table.

"Now what?" she asked.

"I'm going to check out the helm."

"Why?"

"Just to make sure everything's in working order."

"Are we going to leave the marina?"

"Probably not. But I want to be ready if we have to."

She might have asked for clarification but decided to leave the topic alone. He spent several minutes in the captain's chair, checking instruments before starting the engine.

"Does it have fuel?" she asked.

"Maybe three quarters of a tank."

He'd just stepped back to the table when she heard heavy footsteps coming along the wooden deck.

Zane whipped out his concealed pistol so fast that she wasn't sure what she was seeing. He pushed her down on the seat cushion, moved the curtain a fraction, and sat with the weapon trained toward the sound of the approaching steps. Her pulse was pounding as she glanced from the window to Zane and back again. He looked like he was braced for an invasion. But the steps didn't slow and whoever was out there on the dock kept on walking past.

As the sound receded, Zane moved a window curtain farther aside and peered out. "It looks like a guy going to one of the boats at the end of the dock," he said. "But stay down and let me make sure."

He held the gun beside his leg and strode through the door onto the deck. She watched him gazing down the dock. He didn't return for several moments, and she waited with her breath frozen in her lungs.

When he finally stepped back inside, she asked, "Well?" hearing her high, thin voice.

"If he's one of the bad guys, he would have had to be already installed on that boat."

She let out the breath she'd been holding, then glanced at Zane. He'd been gruff with her, but she hadn't realized he was on a knife edge of tension. And she hadn't helped any.

When he sat back down, he left the gun on the table.

She reached to cover his hand with hers. "Sorry."

"For what?"

"I've been acting like a bitch."

"Of course not. You're under a lot of stress."

"Is that an excuse?"

"Yes."

"Why?"

"I've been in a ton of dangerous situations. You haven't. You were just trying to do something good for your father, and you walked into a mess. A murder and then a guy you'd never met before telling you the two of you were meant for each other. It's a lot to deal with, and I wish I hadn't contributed to the situation."

"Well, it's a mixed blessing. I know I can rely on you —totally."

"You can. Always."

For long moments, neither of them spoke. There was so much more she wanted to say to him, but she knew it would have to wait.

Finally she said, "Maybe we were safer at the Ritz-Carlton."

"No, I'd be jumpy there, too. Like every time a maid knocked on the door or someone came in to check the minibar.

He got up and walked around the cabin, closing all the curtains.

"I'm tired of feeling like I have a target on my back," she said.

"Yeah. Like I said to Teddy, I'd be happier if this boat were a cabin in the woods, but that has its disadvantages, too.

"You said you didn't want to just hide out. What's the plan?"

He sighed. "I'd like to get some information from the cops."

"But from the sound of your voice, you think that's too prob-lematic."

"Well, if you said you were the niece of the guy whose house burned down and wanted information, you'd run into problems. You don't want to tell them you were in there and heard guys beating up your uncle, then murdering him. And you don't have any identification. For all they know, you could have read about a rich guy's house getting burned down and now you're working some angle."

"Right," she answered. The conversation was driving home how hard it was for him to investigate her uncle's murder. "But I'm being a pain in the ass," she said.

"No."

"Not even if I want to go to that bar with you?"

To her relief instead of forbidding her to get involved, he said, "Well—we need to set up some ground rules."

11

Zane kept his gaze on Francesca.
 "Okay."

That word of agreement was like ten-pound weights being lifted off his shoulders. She'd been chafing at the precautions he'd insisted on since the escape from the thugs, but the man walking down the dock had served a good purpose. She seemed to have finally gotten the idea that he wasn't laying down edicts to torture both of them.

"What do you want me to do?"

He laughed, the first humor he'd seen in this situation. "Actually, I haven't decided how to work this. Maybe the first thing you should do is get some rest."

She nodded. "That makes sense."

Relieved that she'd agreed, he walked down the companionway. "I'm going to take the room on the dock side, so I can keep an eye on the surroundings.

In his cabin, he closed the curtain, listening as he heard Francesca follow him to the cabins. When he thought she was settled in her bunk, he plugged in his computer to the electrical system on the boat and hooked into the marina's Wi-Fi. First he got a map showing the location of The Tin Man bar and found it was a block away from Tin City. When he opened the Web site he found several pictures.

Like its namesake, the building had corrugated tin walls. The bar itself was located along one of the long interior walls with the lower portion also built of tin. The top was a long piece of native cypress. Industrial light fixtures hung from the ceiling. Additional decor consisted of neon signs advertising various brands of beer. There were no windows. The place did not serve meals, only a variety of cheap snacks.

The tables were unattractive brown plastic with chairs that mostly matched.

What Zane liked best was the large parking lot in front and around the right side. Hopefully, he and Francesca could get a space away from the door but close enough to watch who was coming in and out.

Around six, he checked his weapon and put his windbreaker back on. Of course Florida was an open carry state, but he preferred not to be provocative.

Francesca was lying on her bed. When she looked up at him, he had to stifle the impulse to join her on the horizontal surface.

"I was afraid you were going to leave me here," she murmured.

"I said I'd take you."

"I know . . . but."

He eased onto the side of the bed and reached for her hand. Keeping his voice even he said, "I will never lie to you."

"Thank you."

After a long moment, he asked, "And you?"

She swallowed and was silent for several seconds. Finally she said, "I don't want to, but if it would save your life, I would."

Their eyes locked.

"Okay, I can say the same thing," he answered.

He held her gaze for a few moments longer, then looked away. If he had to lie to her to save her life, it would mean he was thinking he was going to get killed, and he was desperately trying to keep her out of it. That wasn't counting his lie of omission—about the wolf—of course.

"Enough dire talk," he said. "I know where to find the bar, and I've looked at pictures of the interior."

"You said we weren't going in."

"That's right, but I wanted to know the layout, so I need to make a quick visit. Let's sit in the dining area and make some plans."

She followed him down the hall where he set the computer on the table and showed her both exterior and interior views of The Tin Man.

"Not exactly upscale," she murmured.

"Right. I guess that's why a lowlife hit man hangs out there."

"He's a hit man?"

"Well, he's part of the gang that killed your uncle and went after you." He looked at his watch. "We have a little time. Do you want to get something to eat at a restaurant around here before we go over there?"

"Sure. That will solve the problem of what to cook. But let me change into jeans and a dark tee shirt first."

"And a baseball cap," he added.

"I didn't see you buy any the other day."

"I already had a couple with me."

When she'd put on her surveillance clothing and they'd both donned caps, they drove out of the marina and onto the two-lane road, back toward the shopping center.

There were two fast-food restaurants—a burger place and a pizza parlor.

"Which do you want to try?" Francesca asked.

"I'm not much for pizza."

They headed for the alternative. Francesca got a burger with the works and a bottle of iced tea. Zane got three plain patties on buns and bottled water.

"You like meat," she remarked.

"Yes."

"Didn't your mother make you eat vegetables?"

"She knew it was a lost cause."

They took their food to a picnic table under a shade tree overlooking the water.

"It's low-key and relaxing here," Francesca murmured as she looked around at the unassuming setting.

"Yes." Too bad that neither one of them could entirely let down their guard.

He glanced at her before taking his order apart, eating one bun with the three meat patties on it.

She gave him a considering look. "You weren't kidding about the meat part. Cooking for you is going to be interesting."

The comment stopped him cold, and their gazes locked.

"That's assuming a lot," he said.

"I know. But don't you think it's true?"

"Yes." He hoped with all his soul. He reached across the table and took her hand. There was so much more that he wanted to say, but he kept the words locked behind his lips.

They ate the rest of the meal in silence, until she glanced at the buns still sitting on his plate. "A shame to just throw those away."

"There are a lot of birds around here. They'd probably like them."

"It's okay to feed them bread?"

He laughed. "People do it all the time. It's almost a cliché."

"But the restaurant won't like having bird poop around the picnic tables." She tore up the buns and walked twenty yards down the river, where she scattered the bread.

He watched her lithe movements with a longing he hurried to conceal as she returned.

Back in the car again, they headed toward town and stopped at a drugstore along the highway.

"What are we getting?" Francesca asked.

"Burner phones."

"For what?"

"In case we need to communicate."

Her eyes narrowed. "I thought we were staying together."

"Approximately. We might need to separate."

"You won't leave me in the car," she insisted.

"No."

After making that promise, Zane cruised past the bar, casing the joint.

Francesca craned her neck. "There are eleven cars in the lot."

"Okay. And probably other customers could walk here."

He drove to a cross street where he could turn around, then headed back. He was glad to see that the parking lot had two entrances, if they had to make a quick getaway.

The ideal place to park was in a row of spaces along one side that was shaded by a line of trees. Since all the slots were taken, he waited in a nearby spot until a space in that row opened up. Then he backed in, cut the engine and pulled down the sun visors.

"He could already be in there. If he's coming at all," Francesca said

"Yes. I'm going to take a quick look inside."

"You said . . ."

"Briefly," he clarified.

"What's your excuse for going in?"

"To buy a pack of cigarettes." He activated his phone, and she did the same. They both set them to vibrate. Just to make sure everything was working okay, he called her, and they established that the instruments worked.

After slipping the phone into his pocket, he reached for the door handle. "Stay here. And slump down."

"I will." She cranked back her seat and slid down so that only the top of her hat showed.

He got out and strode toward the door of the bar, his feet crunching on the gravel of the lot. Before entering, he stopped and glanced back at the car, feeling a tightness in his chest. He didn't like leaving Francesca here, but it was better than bringing her inside where Tuckerman and one of his cronies could be lurking. He pulled the bill of his cap down a little farther before pushing the door inward.

He'd seen pictures of the interior, but they'd been shot to make the bar as attractive as possible. In person, it looked grungier, and the customers didn't help. Most were men, dressed in tee shirts and shorts or jeans. There were a few women who were similarly dressed in Florida casual. Nobody looked like someone he'd want to meet in a dark alley.

He saw several people eying him as he entered. Probably he was too clean he thought with a silent laugh.

He thanked God that smoking was prohibited inside bars and restaurants, even here. As it was, the liquor, beer fumes, and body odor were almost too much for his werewolf senses in the enclosed space.

Struggling not to cough, he scanned the patrons and didn't see Tuckerman or any of the other men who had been with him. That would have been too easy. Or maybe the guy would have recognized him.

He waited a beat, then crossed to the bar, taking a position near the cash register.

The bartender was serving draft beer to a customer and took his time getting to the newcomer.

"What'll you have?" he asked as he gave Zane an appraising look.

"You got a pack of smokes?"

"What brand?"

He named a popular product.

The man reached under the counter and produced a pack.

Zane paid cash and put the box in his pocket.

"Get you something to drink?"

"No thinks," he answered before turning and heading down the hall toward the bathrooms. He saw an exit down there, but a sign said an alarm would sound if the door was opened. Which meant that if Tuckerman showed up, he'd be coming in the same entrance Zane had used.

He went into the urine-stinking men's room and used the facilities, just in case anyone was keeping track of him.

When he'd finished, he wanted to throw the cigarettes into the trash, but he kept them in his pocket, even though the tobacco smell was getting to him.

A minute later he was stepping out the door and ambling back to the car.

He saw Francesca visibly relax when she spotted him. He stopped at a trash barrel and tossed in the pack of cancer sticks.

"I was starting to get worried," she said as he slid behind the wheel."

"I wanted to seem casual."

"Was—Tuckerman there?"

"No."

"I don't know whether to be glad or relieved."

"I had the same thoughts." He looked over at her, then tipped his own seat back.

"We just wait?" she asked.

"You want to play blackjack?"

She laughed.

He settled down, wondering when the guy usually showed up, if at all. They watched a couple of customers leave and pull out of parking spaces. Several more arrived.

He was considering how long this stakeout was going to take when another car slid into the space directly on his left. The breath froze in his lungs when he saw a big man with short hair, a beefy face, and big hands get out and settle his pants more comfortably around his waist.

Zane would have recognize the bastard anywhere after seeing him tossing trash onto the ground in the park like he was scattering birdseed. It was Tuckerman, and the man was staring right at them.

From the passenger seat, Francesca couldn't see who had gotten out of the car, but she saw Zane's reaction, and her breath hitched.

12

Zane went rigid, except for his right hand which slipped down to the gun under his jacket. For a heart-stopping moment Tuckerman stayed where he was, and Zane got ready to defend them.

Finally the man turned away and started walking toward the bar.

Now Francesca could see the haircut, the broad shoulders.

"That was him, right?" she whispered in a choked voice.

"Yeah."

"He didn't recognize us?" she asked,

"Not unless he's playing it awfully cool."

"He could call for help."

"I think he's just going in there to have a few drinks and maybe chat with his friends,"

"You think he has friends?"

"Acquaintances."

They watched Tuckerman's big feet crunch across gravel. Moments later, he disappeared inside the bar.

"Now what?" Francesca asked.

"We can't go in after him. That's his home turf. We have to wait until he comes out—hopefully sloshed."

He kept his gun out of the holster and slipped it into the side pocket of the car door.

Francesca gave him a nervous look.

"Just a precaution," he answered as he scanned the bar entrance. Would the guy notice that the same car had been sitting in the same spot when he left?

When Zane started the engine, Francesca's head snapped toward him.

"What?"

"I'm moving to another spot, in case he's curious about what we're still doing here."

He pulled out and found a new space about five cars over. Hopefully the guy wouldn't notice that the unobtrusive Chevy had simply shifted locations. Once they were settled again, he said, "I'm going to use some poetic justice on him."

She gave him a questioning look.

"We'll put a tracker on his vehicle, so he won't spot us following."

He went to the case of equipment in the trunk, got out the small device and the controller before coming around to the passenger window.

When she rolled it down, he said, "Keep an eye on the bar. I'll only be a few minutes."

He saw her tense up as she fixed her gaze on the door.

He went back to the scumbag's car, walked to the back, and dropped his keys. As he scooped them up, he bent down to stick the small device under the bumper. He was quickly back to their rental, where he got out the controller and activated the screen. He could see a green dot indicating where Tuckerman's car was.

"When he moves, we can see where he goes." *I hope*, he added silently.

88

They waited, the minutes ticking by, as the thug enjoyed himself at his favorite watering hole.

Zane hoped he wasn't going to come out with a woman—or a friend—which would complicate things.

An hour and a half later, the mobster emerged from the building, not as steady as he had been when he'd gone in. More good news—he was alone.

As their quarry crossed the parking lot, Zane turned toward Francesca. "We'd better make it look like we have a reason to be here—in case he remembers us. Leaning toward Francesca, he pulled her into his arms across the console. It was awkward with the barrier between them, but he cradled her in his embrace as he pressed his cheek to hers and watched Tuckerman head back to his car.

He could feel her heart pounding as he held her, and he wished to hell he'd insisted that she stay on the boat. No, that wasn't true. If she were out of his sight, he'd be worrying about her. At least he knew she was safe.

When he heard the thug's car start up, he moved the controller so he could see the screen. The green dot was moving slowly.

He was thinking he should ease away from Francesca, instead he kept her in his arms. Maybe they both needed the contact because they clung together for several moments. He ached to tip her face up and lower his lips to hers, but he ruled out the kiss. Later, when they had something to celebrate.

"It's working," Francesca breathed as she stared at the screen.

"Yes."

Tuckerman's car had disappeared, but the tracker was sending out signals strong and steady,

"That's what they saw when they were following us?" she asked.

"Yes. Only they were using a phone."

She watched the screen avidly as he turned right onto the avenue, then headed north.

Zane followed for several blocks, staying far enough back so that he couldn't see the thug's car, but he knew the man had turned onto a side street. When Zane reached it, he saw they were in a downscale neighborhood of small, one-story houses, most made of faded stucco in various rainbow colors. Some lawns were well-kept. Others were scraggly, and some properties were piled with trash. Although it was now after midnight, lights were on in some of the houses. Most were dark.

When Tuckerman slowed, Zane speeded up, driving past the car as though he belonged here.

The thug's vehicle had pulled into a driveway at the side of a small yellow house that seemed to be an average-sized dwelling for the area. The yard was full of weeds.

"Now what?" Francesca whispered.

Zane kept going down the street, parking about half a block away. He sat for a few minutes, looking around the area and saw no one out for a midnight stroll.

"We'll walk back," he said.

They climbed out and headed for the yellow house.

"We don't even know if he lives alone," Francesca whispered.

"Unfortunately."

They walked slowly past, Zane on the alert for signs that anyone was paying attention to them.

One light in their target's house was on, and the curtains were open. Zane could see the man walking across a small living room. He stepped into a hall and turned off the living room light.

"I think he's going to bed," Francesca said.

"Uh huh."

They waited for a beat before Zane said, "This is where the phones are going to come in handy."

She gave him a questioning look.

"We're both going to check out the back. If we can see in, you'll stay there, and I'll go back to the front. When you know he's in bed, text me."

"Where will you be?"

"Jimmying the lock on the front door."

"And I'm supposed to stay in back?"

"It's better if I don't have to worry about you while I'm questioning him. Also better if he doesn't see you."

She thought about that for several moments, then nodded.

They moved slowly across the front yard and eased along the side of the house. Because they didn't want to alert the man inside, they couldn't use a flashlight. Zane went first, picking his way carefully along a dirt path. When he kicked something solid on the ground sending a flowerpot careening along the walkway, they both froze. But after several minutes when there was no reaction from inside, they started moving again. Zane reached the end of the wall and turned the corner, then began moving slowly toward the one window where he could see a light.

Motioning Francesca to stay still, he eased along toward the lighted window. Cautiously, he peeked around the edge of the frame through partially open Venetian blinds. He was looking into a room with a double bed, a bedside table with a lamp, and a chest of drawers across the room. On top was a flat screen TV. A dirty beige throw rug completed the decor. The room was empty, but Zane saw more light coming from under a closed door, and he figured the thug was in the bathroom.

He turned and motioned to Francesca. They met about halfway between the window and the corner.

Leaning toward her, he put his mouth close to her ear and whispered, "Keep watch, but stay at the edge of the window. Punch in my number now and activate when you see he's in bed."

He waited while she put the number on the screen. Giving her a thumbs up, he retraced his steps, turned the corner and headed to the front of the house, being careful not to kick the same flowerpot. He stopped in the shadows at the edge of the front yard, scanning the area. As far as he could tell, nobody was paying any attention to the two individuals casing the little yellow house.

He stayed where he was, waiting for her call. Finally he felt his phone vibrate and whispered, "Okay thanks."

After clicking off, he walked to the front door, where he tried the knob. As expected, it was locked, and he used a credit card inserted between the frame and the door to gain entry.

As he slipped inside, Zane drew his gun. Standing in the living room, he waited while his eyes adjusted to the dimmer light. From the bedroom he heard the sound of shots, and froze. Then he realized that the thug was watching a cop show on TV. Good, that would mask his approach to the bedroom. When he was sure he could see where he was going, he followed the same route that Tuckerman had taken.

Glad that the house had some kind of vinyl tile floor rather than squeaky wood, he crossed the living room and walked quietly down the hall. The bedroom door was wide open. He stopped well back in the doorway, his gaze flicking between the man on the bed and the window. Francesca had eased away from the side of the frame. She raised her hand briefly, indicating that she'd seen him step into the room.

The mobster was propped up against the pillows, facing the TV, but he appeared to be dozing.

Zane clicked on the recording function of his phone before waking his quarry with a loud greeting. "Hello, Tuckerman,"

The man whipped to the side, reaching toward the drawer in the bedside table.

"Don't go for a weapon," Zane ordered, or I'll put a bullet in your chest. And nobody will think it's anything but your TV cops and robbers show."

The man went very still, then flopped back against the pillow.

"What do you want?" he croaked.

"Answers."

He saw the thug's lips firm.

"Guys you work with broke into Angelo Lucci's house and killed him. They ended up disabled, and whoever hired them hired you to go after his niece."

Tuckerman blinked and sat up straighter. Unaccountably, he grinned. "You got that all screwed up," he said.

"Set me straight. Who are you working for?"

The grin turned defiant. "Like I'm gonna tell you."

"Why were you following Francesca? What were you paid to do?"

The man didn't answer.

As the sound of shots started up on the TV again, Zane aimed the gun toward the end of the bed near one of the thug's feet and fired into the mattress.

The man screamed. "Jesus Christ, what are you doing?"

"There's more where that came from," Zane growled. Next time I won't miss your foot."

The thug licked his lips, apparently calculating how little he could say and not get shot.

"I wasn't in on the part at the house," he said. "We was hired afterwards to round up the girl."

Zane snorted. "There were two guys at the house and three following her. It was a big operation. Murder and arson."

"It wasn't murder."

"Oh sure. What's your version of events?"

"I'll get in bad trouble if I tell you."

Zane knew the guy was stalling and that he was also afraid. "You're in bad trouble now," he shot back.

"It was a setup, but it didn't go the way it was supposed to."

"What the hell does that mean?"

"I guess you're gonna find out."

Before Zane could work his way through that comment, the whole dynamics of the scene shifted abruptly as one of the large flowerpots from outside came crashing against the window.

Taking advantage of the distraction, Tuckerman pulled the gun from the drawer in his bedside table. He and the man fired at the same time. The thug's aim was off, and his shot hit Zane's left arm.

Zane's bullet went into the man's chest, and he fell back against the pillows.

In the next moment, Zane felt a gun poking into his back. And he knew in a flash of sick realization that someone had come into the house behind him.

13

"You son of a bitch," a gravelly voice growled. "You killed Connie."

Before the newcomer could obliterate Zane's spinal cord, he heard a loud cracking sound, and the man behind him went down.

Whirling, he saw Francesca standing in the hallway and shattered shards of another flowerpot on the floor around the intruder's head.

"Thanks," he said, looking from her to the man on the floor.

"I saw him through the window. I knew it would be too late if I called you on the phone. I didn't know what else to do besides throw something at the window."

"And then you came around in back of him."

She nodded.

"And saved my life," he added, before dragging in a breath and steadying himself. He weighed the pros and cons of searching the house. He wanted to see what he could find, but were the police already on the way? The shots could be mistaken for the TV show, but the flowerpot crashing against the window was another matter. Then there was his arm, which had started to throb. He could move it, and he thought the bullet had missed the bone. But was it still in there, or had it gone through? He'd have to find that out later.

He looked at the dead man slumped on the bed. Zane had shot in self-defense, but he'd also invaded Tuckerman's house, which meant that getting the police involved was a bad idea.

"We'd better get out of here," he said. "Did you touch anything?"

"The doorknob. The flowerpots," she answered.

He gestured toward the shards on the floor. "Wipe off the bigger pieces with your shirt."

As she stooped to comply, he saw that his arm was bleeding. Damn!

When he pulled off his shirt and wrapped it around the wound, she caught her breath.

"You're hurt."

"Not much. Check for blood on the floor."

She made a sound of distress but bent to inspect the place where he'd been standing.

Ignoring the throbbing pain, he turned to the chest of drawers where he found several more tee shirts. He wrapped one over the makeshift bandage he'd already applied to his arm. After using another to wipe the drawer handles, he pulled on the shirt, which was miles too big.

Looking up, he saw Francesca had straightened and was staring at him.

"The floor okay?" he asked.

"I think so," she whispered.

"Let's beat it." Crossing the room, he stepped over the assassin on the floor.

"Who is he?" she asked.

"His housemate. I assume. Maybe one of the other guys who was following us a couple of days ago. But I don't want to stop now and turn him over." Zane reached into the man's pocket. Finding a wallet, he removed it and took it with him.

On the way down the hall, he opened a door and looked into the other bedroom. It was similar to Tuckerman's, with bedclothes in casual disarray, as well as a nightstand, chest and TV.

Knowing they were out of time, Zane turned to Francesca.

"Gotta get out of here."

"I know."

He led her into the living room and out the door.

"Use your tee shirt to hold the knob," he said, hearing the weakness in his voice.

"What about the other flowerpot?"

"Did it shatter after it hit the glass?"

"Yes."

"Leave it."

Francesca gave him a sharp look. "You're going into shock. You need to lie down."

"Yeah," he admitted

She put her arm around him, holding him close, and it was tempting to lean too much of his weight on her. Once outside, they crossed the yard and headed down the sidewalk, hip to hip, two lovers out late, perhaps coming home from a party.

"Anybody looking at us?" he asked.

She surveyed their surroundings as they walked back to their rental. "Not unless they're hiding behind the window curtains."

That was a possibility, of course. He said only, "Okay. Good."

They kept heading toward the car, and he wished he hadn't parked so far away. He had been holding himself together with spit and packing tape, but the tape was beginning to shred. He gritted his teeth, hoping he was going to make it out of the neighborhood under his own power. When they finally reached the Chevy, he unlocked the passenger door and collapsed into the seat, struggling to keep himself from revealing how little reserve he had left.

She gave him a long look. "I guess I'm going to drive."

―――――

Francesca closed Zane's door, walked around the car and climbed into the driver's seat. When she saw he hadn't hooked his seat belt, she reached across him, pulled out a length of shoulder strap and struggled with the metal catch, cursing silently when she couldn't quite snap it into place.

After she finally hooked it, she took care of her own belt and started the engine.

"Turn off the recorder on the phone," he whispered.

"Oh, right."

She closed the app. She had to get out of the neighborhood, but she wished she had a better idea of the way home.

She kept expecting to see police cars coming in the other direction, speeding toward Tuckerman's house. But they were the only ones moving through the early morning hours as she headed toward the highway.

When she cleared the neighborhood, she wondered what she was going to do next. Zane had been driving, and she hadn't been paying a lot of attention to the route. She wasn't even sure if she could get back to the last place they'd been—the bar.

She could feel the burner phone in her pocket. Probably it didn't have a navigational app. But she knew the marina was on a river off the Gulf. What was it called? Cypress Grove? No Cypress Creek. Maybe she could look up the address in a phone book, for all the good that was going to do her.

As she drove slowly west, she kept sliding glances at Zane. He had cranked back his seat and was lying with his eyes closed. Maybe if she kept going toward the coast, she could figure out where to find the marina, but that would be wasting time when she should be seeing how bad his wound was and tending to him.

It made her stomach knot to think about bothering him when he needed to sleep, but she knew she wasn't going to get home without some help.

Angry with herself for being a total screwup, she asked softly, "Are you awake?"

He stirred in his seat and opened his eyes, looking disoriented, but he answered, "Yes."

She dragged in a breath and let it out before admitting, "We went to the bar first. I don't know how to get back to the marina."

"Can you get to Route 41?" he asked in a slurred voice.

"I'm not sure."

"Give me a minute." He winced as he fumbled in his pocket and pulled out his personal phone, not the burner. As she drove, he got his nav app and turned it on. It was already programed for the marina. After setting the phone in the cup holder near the dashboard, he collapsed into the seat.

She looked at his arm. Blood had seeped through the tee shirt bandage, but it wasn't bleeding freely. That must mean the bullet hadn't hit an artery. Making a quick decision, she decided the best thing was to get him back to the boat.

But as she drove, she couldn't stop guilty thoughts from chasing themselves around in her mind. Zane had found her in trouble on the beach near her uncle's house. He'd done everything he could to help her. She'd felt a rush of connection to him, and she knew he'd felt it too.

Now he'd been shot—trying to figure out why the thugs had killed her uncle and why they were after her. It was only because she'd been looking in the window that he hadn't gotten killed by the man who came up behind him. At least she could give herself credit for that. But she hadn't been much help to him otherwise.

In fact, as she contemplated her behavior from his point of view, she saw herself as an ungrateful jerk.

The trip seemed to take forever, and she thanked God when she finally saw the sign for the marina. Guilt was still swirling in her brain as she pulled onto the access road and returned to the spot they'd left in the parking lot. With a sigh of relief, she cut the engine and sat for a moment, glad that she'd actually made it.

At this hour of the morning, everything was dark and quiet, and she saw no lights in the office or in any of the boats, although there were lights along the edges of the dock.

Zane hadn't said a word since he'd put the phone in the cup holder. Pulling into the space hadn't awakened him, and when she touched his forehead, his skin was wet and clammy and his body was shivering. Did he have a fever, or was this just a reaction to the trauma of getting shot?

"We're home," she murmured. "You have to wake up."

His body jerked, and she saw him reaching for his gun.

Quickly, she put her hand on his arm. "It's okay. It's just me. We need to get you onto the boat. I don't think I can carry you."

"Right," he answered, his voice barely audible.

"We have to make sure neither one of us falls off the dock and into the water."

He managed what she assumed was an attempt at a laugh.

She put his phone in her own pocket and came around to his side of the car, where she unbuckled his seat belt.

"There's a first aid kit in my suitcase," he said.

He grunted as she helped him out of the car. When he wavered on unsteady legs, she put her arms around his waist and took as much of his weight as she could. As she pulled him close, she could feel him shivering. She thanked God he'd made it this far, as they climbed onto the dock. It was wide enough for the two of them to walk abreast. But as they started up the boards, she had to keep him from listing toward the water. It was the longest and slowest thirty yards she had ever walked, and when they reached the Lady Slipper, she sighed with relief. But there was still the problem of getting him from the dock to the boat.

"I can't hold you and pull the boat in," she whispered.

"I'll manage." He slumped against a piling.

Hoping he could stay upright for a little while on his own, she pulled on the rope and brought the craft closer. Still, she could picture him pitching into the water as he tried to board.

"Let's sit down," she said, helping him lower himself to the weathered boards. When he'd done that, she climbed onto the bench seat at the edge of the rear deck, then reached for Zane, easing him up and then across the gap between the boat and the dock.

He landed heavily on the bench and sat breathing hard, his shoulders slumped.

"We made it," she breathed.

Lifting his head, he said, "Check to make sure there's nobody else on board."

She hadn't thought of that, but she knew it was an excellent idea. Quickly she turned on some of the battery-powered lights, then inspected the craft, looking into the bedrooms, the head, and into the storage hatch under the prow before coming back for Zane.

"All clear," she reported when she returned.

He'd already made it into the main cabin. Lurching down the companionway, he plopped onto his bunk.

After pulling off his shoes and settling him on the mattress, she rummaged through his tool case for the kit. He'd said it was for first aid. She hoped it was a bit more substantial than that.

In the dining area, she looked through the kit. There was a packet of antibiotic tablets, and she figured he'd better start taking those to ward off an infection.

She helped him sit up on the bunk and gave him a glass of bottled water and two tablets which he took before flopping down again. Then she got to the part she'd been dreading—looking at the wound.

With more water, a little soap, and one of the tee shirt bandages, she started gingerly washing off the blood, watching Zane's face to make sure she wasn't hurting him too much. When the area was clean, she saw that the bullet had gone into the flesh at the outside of his arm, about four inches from the shoulder. There was an entrance wound and an exit wound, so she had to conclude that the bullet wasn't still inside him. Thank you, God.

"The bullet exited?" he murmured.

"Yes."

"You need to put antiseptic on it, then a bandage. When am I supposed to take another pill?"

She looked at the packet. "It's two to start, then one a day for four more days."

When she finished taking care of the wound, he lay back with a soft grunt.

"Sorry," he muttered.

"You have nothing to be sorry for."

"Getting caught."

She made a dismissive sound. "There was no way to know he had a roommate who would be coming home."

"Should have checked the other bedroom."

She would have protested, but sapping his strength by getting into an argument was a dumb idea. If anyone should be sorry, it was her. For dragging him into this in the first place.

"Give me your gun before you go to sleep," she said.

"You know how to use it?"

"Yes. My dad thought that knowing how to use a weapon correctly was an important skill."

Zane upholstered the weapon, and she took it with her as she made another trip around the boat, dousing the few lights she'd turned on.

Returning, she pushed back the curtain that closed off his room and secured it with the tieback. He was still shivering, and she found blankets in the drawers under the bunk and laid them over him.

"Thanks," he murmured without opening his eyes. She longed to get in bed with him and lend him her warmth. But the surface was small and she didn't want to crowd him.

Instead she opened the curtain on her own cabin so she could see him. Really, they were only a few yards away, and she'd be able to get to him quickly if he needed her.

She thought she should stay awake, but that was impossible. Despite the unease she was feeling, she dropped off quickly— only to awaken, she wasn't sure how much later, feeling disoriented. It took only a moment to remember she was on the boat Zane had rented, and he'd been shot.

That reality was brought home when she heard him moan. Leaping out of bed, she crossed the companionway and hurried to his side. In the dim illumination that came in from the overhead lights on the dock, she could tell he was lying on the bunk with his eyes closed. His head was rolling from side to side, and he was saying something. It sounded like *"Taranis, Epona, Cerridwen,"*

The words were strange, not English. They might have been some kind of otherworldly chant, and they gave her a shivery feeling.

"Zane?" she whispered.

He didn't seem to hear her, and the strange syllables coming out of his mouth grated along her nerve endings. It was too dark to see him clearly, but did his face look somehow different? Were the contours changing? To what? Oh Lord, what was happening?

14

Fear zinged through Francesca. What she was seeing and hearing made her feel like she was standing in a cold wind, unable to stop shivering.

Raising her voice, she shouted, "Zane!" At the same time she gripped his good shoulder and shook him. To her vast relief, the chanting stopped and his eyes snapped open. At first it seemed like he had been pulled from the middle of some scene that wasn't part of reality. Then the look in his eyes changed, and he focused on her.

"Francesca?" he croaked.

"Yes."

"What happened?"

"You . . . you were chanting something. It sounded like something from a cult. I was frightened," she said, the words pouring out of her as she watched his expression.

His face contorted as though someone had pounded a fist into his midsection.

"But you woke me before I finished?" he asked urgently.

"I guess. You stopped."

Now relief rearranged his features.

She put her hand on his good shoulder, trying to reassure him, although she wasn't sure of what.

"I was trying to change," he rasped.

"Change what."

"Shit. That's the last thing I should have said."

"Zane, I don't understand any of this."

"I know." He dragged in a breath and let it out.

"Are you in . . . some kind of cult?"

She waited for him to laugh off the question, but he seemed to be considering it.

"No," he finally whispered. He looked like he wanted to say more, but he only gave a quick shake of his head.

She swung her gaze toward the window, seeing the sky starting to turn from black to gray. "You should have another antibiotic."

"Uh huh."

"I'll be right back." She hurried away. Something strange had just happened, but she couldn't figure out what it was.

In the galley, she got the antibiotic plus more bottled water and brought them back.

When Francesca left, Zane struggled to prop himself up on the pillows. Damn. He knew what had happened. He was wounded, and he was having trouble controlling his inner wolf. He was lucky that Francesca had woken him up before he'd finished the chant and she found an animal in bed.

He knew something similar had happened to his brother when he'd been shot escaping from a drug lab in western Maryland. After Knox had told him about it, he'd laughed. He wasn't laughing now.

He tensed as Francesca came back, looking worried.

Clearing his throat, he offered, "Sorry if I scared you."

"I guess you were having a nightmare."

"Yeah."

He was thinking how badly he'd screwed things up. First he'd almost gotten killed at the Tuckerman house. Now he'd almost scared the shit out of Francesca.

Taking the water and the pill from her, he swallowed the medication. She was watching him, and he was afraid she was going to bring up her previous question. Was he in a cult? He'd said, "No," but maybe there was a kind of truth to the question. He couldn't tell her that the men in his family were under an ancient Druid curse—or had been given a gift by the Druid gods, depending on the way you looked at it.

"How do you feel?" she asked.

"Better," he answered automatically. Mostly he was thankful that he didn't seem to have an infection.

"That's good, but I'd better change your dressing."

He waited while she got more bandages and antiseptic, then unwrapped the dressing. They both looked at the arm.

"It's healing fast."

"Yeah." He didn't add that werewolves had excellent powers of recuperation.

She swabbed him with antiseptic and replaced the bandage. When she looked up, he saw something in her eyes.

"What else is on your mind?"

She swallowed. "Yesterday you said the bad guys might assume we left town. After last night, they know we're still here." She swallowed. "Do you think the one I hit with that flowerpot is dead?"

He reached for her hand. "No."

"Why not?"

"Okay. I'm trying to reassure you. The only guy we know is dead is Tuckerman—because I shot him."

"He shot you first. And you have a recording of what

happened on your phone. It shows you didn't go there to kill him —or rob his house. You wanted information."

He sighed. "I don't think the recording alone buys us much. He didn't really admit to murder or arson. If I'd had more time, maybe I could have gotten the truth out of him. We need more proof. And it doesn't help that I took the other guy's wallet. I should have left it and just taken his ID."

"We were in a hurry. Maybe there's something on the morning news programs."

"There's no TV on the boat, but let me fire up my computer and find out."

He'd laid the machine on the shelf at the side of the bunk. She brought it down, and he booted up, shifting so she could sit beside him and see the screen while he found the Web site of a local station. The headline was, *Murder in Quiet Neighborhood. Man and Woman Suspected.*

Beside him, Francesca gasped.

Quickly he scanned the text. Apparently he and Francesca had been spotted leaving the house after gunshots were heard. A neighbor had gone over and found one man dead in bed. Another had been taken to the hospital with blunt force trauma to the head. The apparent motive was robbery. The man who left the house appeared to be wounded, although that had not been confirmed.

Zane cursed under his breath. He hated seeing such a blatant identifying characteristic.

Francesca was as jumpy as he was. "The guy I hit could die. Or he could wake up and say who we are."

"If he wakes up, he's not going to identify us. He'd have to explain how he knows us. And he sure as hell doesn't want to talk about that or his involvement in your uncle's murder."

"Is he one of the men who was chasing us? Or one of the men the big dog mauled on the beach?"

He tried not to wince when she mentioned the dog. Did he

look like a dog, or was she just unable to comprehend that a wolf had been on the beach? Hadn't he told her the animal was a wolf? He wasn't sure.

"Did the guy look like anyone you saw?" he asked her.

"It was the same type. I mean build, haircut. Tough looking."

"I'm assuming he was one or the other. It's unlikely that Tuckerman was involved and his roommate wasn't."

He shook his head. "I'm forgetting we have their pictures."

He booted up his computer and retrieved the photos of the men that he'd snapped at the park.

One was definitely Tuckerman.

"I didn't see the face of the guy behind me."

"And then he was facedown on the floor."

That observation made him want to slap his forehead.

She gave him a questioning look.

"What am I thinking? His wallet's in my pants pocket."

"Right." She retrieved the billfold, and they both inspected the contents. There was a Florida driver's license in the name of Sammy Jackson plus credit cards in the same name. There was also a wad of cash. When she counted the money, they found a little over two thousand dollars.

"Who carries around that much money?" Francesca asked.

"Someone who got paid for an illegal job."

There was nothing else of significance in the wallet.

"I'll get Decorah to check the name."

"What do we do now?"

"Sit tight." He didn't say, *and hope nobody thinks anything suspicious is going on here.*

"I'd better get some groceries." She gave him a questioning look. "Are you willing to start with something easily digested, like chicken soup?"

He sighed. "If I have to. But you'd better be careful about going out."

"Like how?"

"Stick to that local grocery store we passed. Wear a ball cap and pull the brim down. Don't do anything to call attention to yourself."

"Okay."

"Don't take more than a hundred dollars to the store, and don't use anything bigger than a twenty. Put the rest in the suitcase."

She did as he asked, then looked toward the window. "I'll go now. Maybe the store won't be so crowded early in the morning."

"Hopefully."

He watched her get ready to go and approved of her pedal pushers and blue tee shirt. After she left, he lay back against the pillows and closed his eyes for a few moments. He'd like to get himself and Francesca out of town, but he was in no condition to do more than stay in bed and heal, at least for the next twenty-four hours. Plus, the cops might be watching the escape routes.

He reached for his phone to check in with Decorah, then thought better of it. He didn't want to say what had happened on a phone.

Instead he used a secure computer voice line.

As soon as the call went through, Frank Decorah picked up.

"That was you at the murder house last night, right?"

"Unfortunately." He quickly filled in his boss on the night's activities, not sparing the fact that Jackson had gotten the drop on him.

Frank didn't berate him. "How bad is the wound?" he asked.

"The bullet passed through the outer side of my upper arm."

"And you didn't leave any of your blood there?" Frank asked urgently.

"I don't think so. We wrapped my arm in undershirts from Tuckerman's drawer. I guess we'll find out if I missed a drop." Switching topics, he asked, "Can you have Teddy find out some more about him? And the guy Francesca hit with the flowerpot?"

"Yes. And I'll try to keep tabs on the police investigation as best I can."

When they'd exchanged as much information as either of them knew, Zane clicked off and lay back with his eyes closed. He needed to rest, but he couldn't relax until he knew Francesca was safely back on the boat.

When she stepped off the dock, Francesca turned and glanced at the houseboat. It looked so innocent floating there. Would you ever guess that the couple involved in a break-in and murder last night were hiding out onboard? Well, the guy was. The woman was going out to get some food. As she walked the short distance to the parking lot, she scanned the area, trying to take the kind of precautions that Zane would. Nobody else was around.

Once in the car, she headed for the small shopping center where they'd seen the grocery store. It was less than a mile away, and she wasn't going to get lost on the short trip.

The strip mall wasn't like anything she'd seen back home. It had a strange mix of stores besides the grocery and the restaurants, there was a women's clothing shop, an appliance store, a place that sold seashells, and a cigar store.

A TV was playing in the window of the appliance shop, and a picture of a newscaster standing in front of a house caught her attention. Francesca realized with a little gasp that it was the house where she and Zane had gotten into a lot of trouble the night before. She couldn't hear what the woman was saying through the window, but as she looked more closely she saw crime scene tape on the door of the house.

The images shook her. Obviously the murder was the big news around here.

She walked away quickly, feeling like she should rush back to the boat and tell Zane. But what was there to report, really? She had considered making a pot of chicken soup they could both enjoy, but she changed her mind when she stepped into the medium-sized grocery store.

The layout was unfamiliar, and she didn't know where anything was located. Instead of trying to gather all the ingredients for anything homemade and cooking it in an unfamiliar galley, she went to the aisles with canned goods, picking up chicken noodle soup, beef stew, and a couple of other staples.

What else should she get? Probably something for herself, but she wasn't all that hungry. Still, she had to eat, so she headed for the deli department and selected a couple of ready-made chicken sandwiches. Because she knew Zane liked meat, she also put several packages of cold cuts into her cart.

When she returned to the front of the store, she saw there was only one checkout counter open, and she had to wait behind several women with full baskets who chatted with a hefty redheaded lady working the cash register and bagging groceries. Each transaction seemed to take a century, and she wanted to scream at everyone to hurry up.

Clenching her teeth, she kept her cool, and finally got to the front of the line.

The women in front of her had seemed to know the checker. Maybe a stranger could just transact her business and get out of there quickly.

But when Francesca approached the register, the woman, whose name tag said "Louise," asked, "You new in the neighborhood, honey?"

Francesca's mouth had turned so dry that she could barely speak. *Act normal* she warned herself. "We're vacationing in the area."

"You and your husband. Or do you have kids?"

Francesca dragged in a breath. "The four of us."

Louise looked at the food on the moving belt. "You're not getting much."

"We brought a lot of stuff with us. But Henry asked for the soup, and Josh wanted the stew," she said, wondering how long it would take to ring up her purchases.

"You got a store card?"

"No. I'm paying in cash."

"You can fill out a form."

"No thanks. I'm in a hurry." She dug out a couple of bills and paid. Relieved to be out of the store, she headed back to her car.

The TV was still on in the appliance shop. She wanted to march on past, but she couldn't help stopping when she saw the newscaster still standing in front of Tuckerman's house. Then the scene grew dark, and she stared at what appeared to be a cell phone video. It showed a man and a woman from the back, staggering together down the sidewalk.

Oh my God. It was them—from last night. They stopped beside a car. The man, who looked sick or injured, got into the passenger seat. The woman went around to the driver's side.

The only good news was that it was dark and the video was taken from the back.

As the car started up, the focus switched to the license plate. Her heart stopped, then started to drum inside her chest. Looking over toward their rental, she saw the same license number as though it were in a flashing neon sign.

15

Oh God. Oh God. Somebody last night had taken a picture of the car—even though they'd parked well down the street. And that wasn't all the bad news. Her head snapped up when she saw movement from the corner of her eye. A man who had been in the store looked from the TV to her Chevy.

Her heart was blocking her windpipe as she climbed in the vehicle, tossed the grocery bag onto the passenger seat, and started to back out of the space. A horn loudly sounded, and she slammed on the brakes, narrowly missing a collision with a jeep that was barreling along the access lane. The driver leaned out and hurled a curse at her, and she hoped he wasn't going to pull out a gun.

As soon as the jeep passed, she headed back toward the marina, praying that nobody was following her. She wanted to scream. She wanted to speed back to the houseboat. Instead she drove at a normal pace, checking in the rearview mirror every few seconds to make sure nobody was trailing her.

As he waited for Francesca to return, Zane kept looking at the time on the bottom right of the computer screen. Finally he sighed and forced himself to stop obsessing. Francesca still had the burner phone from last night. He could call her and find out if everything was okay.

The only thing that stopped him was knowing she'd think he didn't trust her to make a simple run to the grocery store.

He knew he should take the opportunity to rest, but he couldn't relax. Instead he kept his ears peeled for the sound of her returning.

Finally, he heard footsteps on the deck. Someone walking fast.

He grabbed his gun and pushed himself out of the bunk, standing on unsteady legs so he could see who was coming.

It was Francesca.

When she pelted across the main cabin and down the stairs, he was pretty sure something was wrong. Her wide-eyed look confirmed it. As her gaze zeroed in on the gun, she made a strangled sound.

He lowered the weapon. "What?"

"Someone took a cell phone video of us on the sidewalk last night. From the back. You don't see our faces, but it shows us getting into the car. And it shows the license plate."

"Where the hell did you see that?"

"On a TV in the appliance store."

"Shit." He backed into his room and sat down heavily on the bunk. "There wasn't anything about that on the news earlier."

"I guess they hadn't come forward with it yet. Or maybe they didn't turn it over to the cops. Maybe they sold it to the TV station."

He considered. "Did anyone notice you—or the car?"

She flapped her arm in frustration. "A guy was looking at the plate. And the checker in the grocery store asked me a bunch of nosy questions."

"You didn't tell her where we were staying?" he demanded.

"No. I pretended we were vacationing with our kids. But how many places are there around here to stay? All they have to do is start looking for the car."

He cursed again. "We'd better split. But we can't take a chance on driving with those plates. I guess the only good news is that I used my alternate ID to rent the car." He didn't say that their fingerprints were in the vehicle.

He sat for a moment gathering his strength. Was it better to leave the Lady Slipper here as a decoy and take the dinghy on the platform off the back? He decided to leave the dinghy in place and take the larger boat, since there was no telling how far they'd have to travel and under what conditions.

"Go to the main room and keep watch. Tell me if you see anyone coming."

Francesca gave him a long look. "You should be lying down."

"Later." As she started for the stairs, he called up a map of the area, checking the waterways and plotting an escape route.

Which was better, to head into the Gulf or take this river inland? And what about the fuel? How far could they get on what was in the tank? Should he take a chance and stop at the fuel pump? Or should he just head out?

Finally he decided not to delay leaving. Opening his medical kit, he reached for a small pill bottle with some emergency doses of amphetamine. He knew that taking one in his condition was risky. But if he couldn't function well enough to get them out of here, the game was up. They'd be in jail trying to explain to the cops why he'd had to shoot Tuckerman in self-defense. And the cops would tell him a home invader couldn't claim he had to shoot to keep from getting killed.

Clicking on the secure communications system, he sent a message to Decorah explaining briefly what had happened. Then he headed for the helm.

Francesca turned around as he came up the stairs, trying to look like he was steady on his feet and fit to pilot a cabin cruiser.

"You see anything?" he asked.

"A pickup truck stopped on the access road. Do you think they're looking for us?"

"I hope not."

He wished he could ask someone else to cast off. Or do it himself. But in his current condition, he lacked the agility to get off, untie the boat, and scramble back on. He'd probably fall into the gap between the boat and the dock.

Giving Francesca a direct look, he said, "You'll have to get off and undo the lines. Do the one at the bow first and toss it onto the front decking. Then do the stern, and hold the rope while you climb back aboard—quickly. The lines are secured to cleats. There's a loop at the end. Undo it and then unwind the rest of the rope.

She looked uncertain but said, "Now?"

"Yes. When you're aboard, toss the lines onto the decks. And also unplug the electrical connection to the marina. Leave the cord on the deck."

His heart raced as he watched her climb off and felt the boat rock while she fumbled with the electric line and then the cleat and the rope at the bow. Then came the harder part. From the pilot's seat, he couldn't see her detaching the aft rope. But he felt the cruiser dip to the side as she plopped onto the rear deck. Thank God she'd made it.

"Okay, he called out?"

"Yes."

He swivelled around to see her hurrying into the main cabin, limping slightly.

His breath caught when he saw her. "What happened?"

"I banged my shin getting back on."

"Jesus, I'm sorry. I should have done it."

"Not when you were shot yesterday."

He sighed. "Right. Keep a lookout while I get us out of here."

It was years since he'd actually piloted a boat. And in truth, the one he'd lived on while going after the smugglers was a lot smaller than the Lady Slipper. But he got the craft out of the slip and started down the river, heading away from the Gulf.

Francesca was in the cabin in back of him.

"You see anymore activity up on the road?" he called.

"No. Just the one pickup.

That was something, anyway. And there was more good news. The cops were looking for a couple. Nobody had seen him at the grocery store. And nobody had seen her at the marina office. Plus, she'd made up a story about being here with their kids. If they were lucky, nobody would realize they were the man and woman involved in last night's armed robbery and murder. He winced as he put it that way, but that was the way the cops would see it—until he could prove otherwise. And while he was trying to do it, Francesca would be in danger. There were too many cases where bad guys had used a jail inmate to murder a fellow prisoner.

There was one more fact he couldn't work his way around. The car with the telltale license plate was in the marina lot. Probably it was only a matter of time before someone discovered it. But all he could do about that was put as much distance as he could between themselves and the car.

The river was maybe seventy-five yards wide, with tropical vegetation on either side. Ordinarily he would have appreciated the greenery and the water birds roosting in the trees. Now it was all he could do to stay on the right side of the waterway and not hit the bank or any of the docks sticking into the water. Many had boats moored to the pilings or to cleats like the ones which had kept the Lady Slipper tied up at the marina. Houses peeked from the greenery beyond the docks. None looked like a luxury residence—just the homes of ordinary people who'd bought property on the river when it was affordable.

Occasionally they passed another craft on the water, most of them small speedboats.

After a few hours, Zane could feel the amphetamine wearing off, but he knew he'd be crazy to take another one. He gritted his teeth, wondering how long he could sit here piloting the boat. When Francesca came up behind him and rubbed his shoulders, he leaned into the caress.

"What can I do? Can I take your place at the wheel?"

He considered the offer. "Have you ever steered a boat?"

"No."

"Better let me do it."

She came around and looked into his eyes. "I think you can't push yourself much farther."

"I think you're right," he answered wearily, considering their next move. Consulting the computer map, he saw that they were skirting the edge of a wildlife area. If they took one of the tributaries that appeared from time to time, they'd move into the nature preserve. Once away from civilization, they could pull up under vegetation overhanging the river.

Previously he'd thought about tying up at an unoccupied dock, but he knew he could still run into the homeowners. Now he liked the idea of getting away from civilization.

With that in mind, he took the next tributary he encountered. It was only about fifty yards wide and narrowed as they rode upriver. There were no houses here, and the vegetation on either side of the water looked a lot like untamed jungle. When he came to a spot where overhanging branches of a mangrove would partially hide the Lady Slipper, he cut the engine and sagged back into his seat.

Turning to Francesca, he asked, "Could you tie us up? She climbed out onto the front deck and threw the rope over a tree branch, pulling the end back to the Lady Slipper and knotting it. It wasn't a very seamanlike job, but what did it matter?

She did the same with the rope in the stern, then came back to him, obviously evaluating his condition.

"I've got the groceries I picked up at the store. You need to eat. I'll heat up chicken soup for you. And if that agrees with you, I bought a bunch of lunch meat."

"Thanks." Too bad he wasn't in shape to go hunting.

Francesca brought him a mug of soup. It was the last thing he wanted to eat, but he dutifully swallowed most of it.

Probably he should lie down, but it was too much trouble to get up. He slumped down in the chair, and closed his eyes—just for a few minutes.

He wasn't sure how much later he was awakened by a feeling that something was wrong. Struggling to clear his mind, he dragged in a breath, taking in the humid air of the river, trying to figure out what had triggered his unease. Did he hear something in the darkness? A stealthy movement?

Could someone have followed the Lady Slipper from the marina—or figured out where they'd gone? In the next moment he snapped to attention when he heard the sound of a heavy body hitting the back deck. It sounded like a large animal that had leaped from the tree where they were tied up.

Instantly on alert, but still shaky, he reached for the gun he remembered setting on the floor beside his chair.

The weapon wasn't there. Francesca must have taken it for defense when she saw he was asleep.

Moving slowly, he swivelled the pilot's chair around to face the open doorway at the back of the cabin. As he stared into the darkness, he saw a long, lean, light-colored shape glide across the deck. In a flicker of movement, a pair of glowing green eyes zeroed in on him.

From the eyes and the predatory way the beast moved, he knew it was a big cat. It must have come out of the natural area, started sniffing around the boat, and jumped down from a tree branch for a closer look.

He studied the creature. It was perhaps five feet long, excluding the tail, and something over a hundred pounds. As he watched, it took a cautious step toward the open door of the cabin. When it hissed, Zane wondered what he was going to do now—without a weapon.

But even if he'd had the gun, he didn't want to shoot this animal whose territory he'd invaded. It looked like a Florida panther, and from his reading he know there were only about three hundred of them left in the wild.

Although his thinking processes were muzzy from sleep and his recent wound, he knew one thing. A man would be no match for the big cat's teeth and claws. But a wolf could intimidate this animal.

With no other choice for self-defense, he glanced over his shoulder, satisfied that the animal's arrival hadn't awakened Francesca. Praying she'd stay in her cabin, he softly began the chant of transformation. At the same time, he pulled off his shirt, then his pants and finally his underwear, tossing the clothing onto the deck.

As he began to make the change from man to wolf, his bandage dropped to the varnished board, and the wound in his arm twanged. He came down on all fours, feeling the freedom of his hidden self.

The panther was standing stock-still on the deck, probably confounded by what it had just witnessed. But when the wolf took a slow step forward, the cat's fur fluffed up, and its tail swished. Making a hissing sound, it backed up.

Zane's bold posture was a bluff. He was in no shape to tangle with the cat's sharp teeth and claws, but he hoped his aggressive behavior would be deterrent enough.

They faced each other across the deck, Zane slowly padding forward and the cat backing up.

Zane growled deep in his throat, warning the invader that this boat was his domain and he would defend it.

The cat was almost to the back of the deck. What now? When Zane took another step forward, the panther leaped. The wolf tensed, but instead of landing on him, it sprang into the tree, shaking the branches as it scrambled into the darkness.

Zane breathed out a sigh of relief. His total focus had been on the cat. Now that the danger was over, he heard a sound behind him. Hairs bristling on his back, he slowly turned to find Francesca standing inside the cabin, the gun in her hand, pointed at him.

16

Other than the bristling hairs, Zane stood frozen in place, staring at the wide-eyed woman with the gun. His life mate. Or was she going to put a swift end to the relationship?

It flashed through his mind that his own decisions had catapulted him into this mess. Like, maybe he should have come clean with her about the rescue on the beach. Now she didn't know Zane Marshall was the dangerous-looking wolf standing on the deck facing her. He couldn't talk, couldn't tell her it would be a bad mistake to shoot him. And the idea of transforming in front of her made his stomach tie itself into knots.

He looked into her eyes, trying to read what she might be thinking. Did he detect a glimmer of understanding? On some unconscious level, did she recognize him? And was that good or bad?

What if he dropped to the deck and rolled over like a big old dog? Would that demonstrate that the wolf was no threat?

That image made him cringe.

With the river behind him and Francesca with a gun in front of him, he did the only realistic thing he could think of at the moment. He leaped over the side, hitting the water with a tremendous splash.

He went down like a rock, sinking down, down below the surface into the murky depths where he struggled to hold his breath. Finally to his relief, he began to come up again.

Was Francesca looking over the side, trying to spot him? He struggled not to break the surface until he had swum to the prow. The wolf couldn't grab onto anything. All he could do was lean against the wooden hull, dragging in air and silently saying the chant that would change him back into a man.

When he was human again, he dragged in a breath and called out. "Don't shoot. I'm coming around to the deck."

He swam back and reached to grab hold of the gunwale. With an effort he hauled himself aboard and sat dripping like a wet fish on one the cushions.

Francesca still held the gun. He hoped it was to scare away the panther if it came back.

She stood unmoving, staring at him. "Are you going to tell me you were already in the water when that wolf went over the side?"

He kept his gaze steady. "I might have tried that. You've just made it clear that wouldn't do me any good."

"All that crap you told me about your family. An ancient curse, was it?"

"An ancient bargain with the Druid gods."

"Oh right."

"Could I put on some clothes before we have this discussion? You know, before I catch my death of cold."

She winced, probably remembering that he'd been shot yesterday. "You can get dressed," she said in a low voice. She looked at his arm which was now oozing blood again. "Wash the river water off your wound and slather some antiseptic on it."

He crossed the deck, leaving wet footprints on the varnished boards. In the head, he stepped under the shower and quickly washed himself. After drying off, he applied antiseptic, and pulled on a tee shirt and jeans. When he was dressed, he realized he should have cut a couple lengths of bandage before he showered.

Using his other hand and his teeth, he wrapped some gauze around his arm and managed to tie it off. Luckily it was at the end of the roll, and he didn't have to try and cut it.

He'd delayed as long as he could, but he knew he had to face Francesca. Stiff-legged, he returned to the main cabin where she was sitting at the table. At least she didn't move when he sat down opposite her. And she had put the gun on the table between them.

The tone of her voice and her next question were less reassuring. "You said you wouldn't lie to me. What did you tell me that was true?"

He wanted to flinch away, but he kept his own gaze steady. "About us, or about your uncle's murder?"

"You can start with my uncle."

The tension buzzing between them made him feel like an animal caught in a net, but there was nothing he could do about it besides give her honesty.

"Everything I said about the case is true—as far as I know. I've been trying to protect you and trying to figure out what's going on. There's stuff that doesn't add up. I mean, if you want the truth, I feel like somebody's playing games with me —with us."

"What makes you think so?"

"The way Tuckerman confronted me. He was protecting some secret, but I don't know what. Unfortunately, the other guy came in before I could get any answers. And now we're prime murder suspects."

She ignored that last part and asked, "And us?"

He felt as though razor wire were twisting in his guts. But he said only, "The moment I held you in my arms on the beach, I felt . . . connected to you."

She snorted. "Tell me again about men in your family bonding with their life partner."

He raised one shoulder. "I suppose it's to make sure that we find . . ." He almost said mates. "Wives."

Maybe she caught the slight hesitation, but his only option was to continue. "The Druid gift from the gods is ancient. I imagine that in ages past . . ." He stopped, then forced himself to say, "Werewolf men were pretty savage."

Her only response was a clenching of her teeth.

"We're housebroken now." When she didn't respond to the joke, he went on, "Every werewolf is an Alpha male, the head of his own pack. Until recently, they didn't get along with each other, but we've learned to work together. Several of us are Decorah Security agents."

"You're holding something back," she bit out. Then with sudden insight she asked, "Do you say some kind of chant to change into a wolf?"

"Yes. An appeal to the Druid gods."

"Like the other night. Only I stopped you?"

"Yes."

"Can I hear it?"

He gave her a hard look. "Only if you want to be sitting across from a wolf."

"No. Tell me what else I don't want to hear."

He sighed. "There were some . . . bad aspects to our reality. The trait is sex linked, so only male babies lived. And when a youth went through puberty, he'd have to change to wolf form for the first time. About half of them died."

Her look of horror made him go on quickly, "My cousin Ross is married to a geneticist. She solved the problem of the girl babies. She figured out how to save them, although so far none of them has acquired the ability to change shape."

Again he left the words hanging between them.

"What the hell do you want me to say?" he challenged.

"I don't know. No, okay, wait—do I have free will? Can I walk away from you, if I want?"

"I don't know." Maybe she could do it. And if she did, it might kill him.

They sat in silence for several more minutes. Finally she asked, "If you'd had the gun, would you have shot the panther?"

"The idea of killing it made me sick. I might have shot into the air to frighten it. Without the gun, I hoped the wolf could scare it off because I wasn't in any condition to fight."

Once more, she didn't respond.

His body felt leaden. It was almost too much effort to keep sitting at the table. Adding to the weight pressing down on him was the knowledge of just what a mess he'd made.

Finally, he simply couldn't cope with the effort of staying upright in the chair. "I've had a rough day and night," he said. Before she could say the same he turned and headed for his cabin, struggling to stay on his feet. He almost tripped on the stairs and only managed to stay upright by grabbing the railing. It wasn't just that he'd reached the limit of his physical resources, it was the knowledge that he'd probably driven away the woman who was his mate.

Could a werewolf recover from that? He had no way of knowing. It was another nasty topic that the clan didn't discuss.

He kept a tight grip on the railing, as much to keep his balance as to anchor himself to reality. When he reached his cabin, he drew the curtain and stopped beside the bunk. Swaying slightly on his feet he pulled off his shirt and tossed it onto the end of the bed. He left his pants on and eased himself onto the bunk, being careful not to put any pressure on his wounded arm.

17

Francesca watched the slump of Zane's shoulders as he walked unsteadily toward the stairs. When he started to fall, she was out of her seat, but he caught himself and made it to the lower level.

She closed her eyes, sitting very still, listening to the buzzing of insects and the slapping of water against the side of the boat.

Probably the panther wouldn't come back. But what else was out there? She didn't know, but she had a better appreciation of the dangers of the tropical night.

They were less terrifying than the dangers inside this boat. It was personal danger of a type that she never could have imagined in a thousand years of nightmares. A werewolf was a creature of myth and legend, a creature to be feared. And here she was trapped as consort of one of those frightening beings. She had sensed power in Zane that she couldn't explain. Now she understood.

She shuddered.

Zane had said he was drawn to her since the first moment he'd held her in his arms. If she admitted it, the same was true for her. He, at least, had realized what was happening. She had been clueless—except for the zings of feeling that had kept assaulting her since the night of the fire.

And now what? Could she walk away from him? She tried out that idea and felt a terrible sense of loss—and panic. He'd said she was his life mate. Did she have a choice about that? Or was she now under the same ancient Druid spell that held him captive?

The past few days scrolled through her mind like a video tape focusing on everything she had done. Everything Zane had done.

She'd given him a hard time, probably because she'd been frightened, and she hated relinquishing control of everything, even when she'd recognized that Zane was far better equipped to deal with her problems than she.

Still, she'd told him all her secrets, and he had told her none of his.

She made a low sound. She'd thought hers were bad. His were an order of magnitude greater. Beyond imagining until a few minutes ago. Lord, if the government knew about his abilities, they'd probably put him in a cage and try to figure out how to make a weapon out of him.

She shuddered, yanking herself away from that line of thinking and back to Zane Marshall as a man.

He might not have shared his . . . his shape-shifter secret. But since the moment she'd met him, he had done everything he could to try and save her life. For his efforts, he'd gotten shot and become a murder suspect. Then he'd pushed himself to the limit getting the two of them out of the marina and down the river.

And probably he was in his bunk, thinking she was going to walk away from him as soon as they cleared themselves of the murder charges—if they could. She shuddered, wondering if there was any way to convince the cops that they were only trying to find out who killed her uncle and why.

She wanted to stop being a fugitive. And what else? What did she want the rest of her life to be?

For long moments she sat with her elbows on the table and her chin cradled in her palms. Finally she picked up the gun from the table and started toward the back of the boat.

As the curtain closing off Zane's cabin slid back, he looked up to see Francesca standing in the doorway holding the gun.

"You're going to have another try at it?" he mumbled, thinking he shouldn't have left the weapon on the table.

"Yes," she answered, her voice softer than he could have imagined after their talk in the main cabin.

She checked the safety, then reached over to lay the semi on the shelf above the bed before perching on the side of the bunk.

He had been lying in the middle of the mattress, trying to simply turn off his brain so that he could get some sleep. Well, that was impossible now.

"Give me some room," she whispered.

He scooted over a little so that she could wedge herself into the space along the edge, turning to her side and pressing tight against him.

He didn't move, didn't let himself think about why she had come here. She didn't speak again, and he felt his heart begin to pound as he waited for what might come next.

She lay with her head against his shoulder while she reached to trace the shape of his lips, then play her fingers over his chest, touching his nipples before finding more neutral areas.

He had thought he was too worn out to respond, but his breath caught, then caught again as she hitched up, stroking her mouth against his, just the barest whisper of a kiss that sent heat flaring to the farthest reaches of his body.

Then her tongue was stroking against the seam of his lips, and he opened for her, feeling her explore the line of his teeth and the sensitive tissue just beyond.

He wanted to hold her there, keep her where he could marvel at the wonderful taste of her and the pressure of her body against his hip. But when he started to raise his arm, she circled his wrist with her thumb and index finger.

Grasping his wrist with one hand, she used the other to undo the button at the top of the jeans he'd hastily put on after his shower. Ignoring his questioning look, she finished with the button, then slowly lowered the zipper of his fly.

She had already aroused him with her touches and kisses. He caught his breath as she reached inside the jeans and closed her fist around his cock. That was enough to make him feel like he might go off like a rocket.

When she released him, he heard himself make a moaning sound. And when she climbed off the bed, he wanted to plead with her to come back. Instead she stood beside the bunk and pulled her shirt over her head before unhooking her bra and tossing it away.

As she stood before him, she lifted her breasts in her hands. The nipples were already hard, and she took them between her thumbs and fingers, playing with them as she kept her gaze locked on him.

He could barely breathe as he watched her. Next she undid her pants, skimmed them down her legs along with her panties.

Naked, she stood looking down at him before reaching to pull off his pants.

He lay in the bed, fully aroused, struggling to keep from begging for more. She didn't make him wait for long. His heart leaped as she climbed back onto the bed. Her movements decisive, she straddled him, bring him inside her in one smooth motion.

For long moments she stayed poised on the knife edge of possibility, and he forced himself not to thrust his hips upward as her eyes locked with his.

Her first movements were slow, teasing. And when she began to move faster, he kept pace with her, his breath coming in gasps as she brought him higher and higher to a peak of pleasure he had never imagined. He grasped her buttocks with the hand of his good arm, anchoring her to him, holding back until he thought he would reach his breaking point. When he felt her contract around him, he let go, his shout of pleasure vibrating through the small cabin.

They were both slick with sweat and breathing hard as she shifted off of him and flopped onto the mattress.

He brought his uninjured arm up so that he could stroke her damp hair back from her forehead. Pushing himself up, he looked down at her.

His throat was so constricted that he could barely speak, but he managed to ask, "Why, exactly did you come back here?"

"Out in the main cabin, I started thinking about what kind of man I wanted to spend my life with. I wanted someone steady, honest, loving, a man with principles. And when I thought about the past few days, I realized you were all of those things. Everything about you is right—except for one scary detail."

"The big bad wolf?"

"Yes. But I guess I'm getting used to that, too." She cleared her throat. "And your weird diet. Werewolves don't drink coffee?"

"Any drugs play havoc with our systems."

"And I guess I'm not going to be making you a lot of salads."

He laughed, astonished at the one-eighty turn their relationship had taken.

Closing his eyes, he knitted his fingers with hers. They were in a hell of a mess, and he wasn't sure how he was going to get them out of it. But for the moment he felt a kind of peace—and completion—that he had never before experienced in his life. His brother and cousins had never told him about this—but he knew they would have been embarrassed to reveal so much.

"Thank God," he murmured. "I was thinking about what I was going to do if you walked away from me. Of course, I still have to figure how we're getting out of this mess."

"You work for a detective agency, don't you? Can't they help us?"

He sighed. "They were providing support. I called them when you were at the grocery. But I've been busy since then."

He pushed himself up and reached for the burner phone that he'd set on the shelf next to his laptop. When he punched in the Decorah Security number, the phone was answered on the first ring—by Frank Decorah, who must have been at the office all night.

"Zane? Is that you?"

"Yes."

"What the hell is happening down there? You went silent after we last talked."

Zane sighed. "Sorry. We were dealing with a situation." Quickly he filled in his boss on Francesca's trip to the grocery store and their departure from the marina.

"Are you all right?"

He sighed again. "Still recovering from the gunshot wound. Do you have any information on the other one—the guy who Francesca hit over the head to save my bacon?"

"He's recovering in the hospital, but he's refusing to say anything."

"Maybe if he talked, the cops would get a better idea of the whole picture. Meanwhile, we're murder suspects, and I don't know how to get the hell out of the state."

Teddy Granada, who was apparently also on the line, spoke

up. "I can home in on your GPS signal. You're on a tributary of the Augustine River?"

"Yes."

"And I saw a shot of your backs as you walked down the sidewalk. Nice that everybody in the world has a cell phone camera."

Zane made a sound of agreement.

"You appear to be in a swamp," Teddy said, switching back to the current problem.

"It was the best I could do last night when I was falling asleep at the wheel. We had to get out of the main traffic lane." He glanced at Francesca and then away.

"Understood," Frank answered.

"Our car is back at the marina, and we can't risk using it in any case. Also I didn't want to take the gamble of stopping to fuel up, so we don't have much gas left."

"You have a plan?" Frank asked.

"I was thinking about something. Maybe it will work and maybe it won't."

"Let's hear it," Frank prompted.

After listening to what Zane had in mind, Frank approved, with one caution. "We can't get an operation like that up and running for at least twenty-four hours."

"Understood."

"Sit tight. We'll let you know the location—and the timing."

Zane clicked off and turned to Francesca. "We're going to have to stay here for at least a day."

"And do what?" she asked.

He shook his head regretfully, "How about—pray that nobody figures out where we might have gone and comes up this tributary looking for us?"

"You have a way of dampening my enthusiasm for a little R and R." She gave him a considering look. "I guess we have to keep watch, but you should let me take the first shift. And you

133

have to eat something. Do you think you could choke down any more of that chicken soup?"

Now that the wolf was no longer a secret, he said, "I'd rather go hunting in the swamp."

"I'd rather not worry about you out there."

"Point taken." His voice turned serious. "That panther could come back. I don't want you out on the deck."

"Yes."

Francesca took the gun out to the main cabin. Zane joined her just after noon.

"I take it there were no problems," he said.

"A couple of times I heard a boat in the distance, but nobody came up this way."

"Good." Zane sat down in the pilot's chair. "You get some sleep. I'll stay here—hoping a nice juicy snake drops onto the deck so I can eat it."

"Would you?"

"Doesn't everybody say snake tastes like chicken?"

She made a face. "I'm not going to find out."

"You would if you were hungry enough," he answered, glad that they were relaxed enough to banter.

"I've still got stuff from yesterday."

"The power to the fridge is off."

"But nobody's opened the door. It should be okay."

She ate a sandwich and washed it down with bottled water before heading back to her bunk.

Zane kept watch, listening to the sounds of the untamed area. He was feeling remarkably better, and he wished he could slip off into the swamp, but he wasn't going to leave his mate unprotected.

Early the next morning, his phone rang. It was Frank. "You can start heading toward the marina on the other side of the swamp," he said.

"Let's hope the Lady Slipper can get through."

Francesca, who had heard the phone, came up the stairs and stood by the cabin door. "Are we ready to leave?" she asked when he clicked off the call.

"Yes."

"Thank God. This waiting is nerve-wracking."

He crossed to her, taking her in his arms and simply holding her. He'd hated being so close and yet unable to be with her. Now he couldn't stop himself from enjoying her body pressed to him.

She raised her face, and he lowered his head, so that their lips met. Instantly he felt so aroused that his head spun. His hands moved over her, her ribs, her hips, the sides of her breasts. She moaned and eased the top part of her body away from him so that he could cup her breasts through her shirt. Reaching around to her back, she unhooked her bra and pulled it out of the way.

He swept her shirt and bra upward, bending to find one hardened nipple with his mouth, while his fingers played over its mate.

"God yes," she sobbed, clasping her hands around the back of his head.

She had already kicked off her pants and panties when he lifted her onto the table, freeing his cock before stepping between her legs and plunging into her.

They both gasped at the intimate contact. He pulled back and pressed forward again, compelled to rush toward completion even while he was trying to keep himself from coming in the next few seconds, but she was right with him, pushing for her climax as they rocked wildly together.

They exploded in a fiery burst of ecstasy, both of them gasping for breath as they clung together.

She lifted her head, staring up at him, her eyes reflecting the depths of the emotions he felt.

"That's what it's like to make love with a wolf?" she asked.

"Only when he's doing it with his mate," he managed to say.

"It was never like that for you before?"

"Not hardly."

"Well, I can certainly say the same."

She kept her arms around him, holding him to her. But finally he kissed her once more and eased away.

She gave him a long look. "I guess you're feeling better."

He grinned. "Apparently. I'd like to see if I could last a little longer, but we have to leave."

"I know. But let me get cleaned up first."

He nodded, admiring the curve of her butt as she picked up her clothing from the deck and scurried for the stairs. He wanted to follow her, but he knew he had to stick to business.

She was back a few minutes later, dressed in a fresh tee shirt and cutoffs. "How far are we going?" she asked.

"Under five miles, I think." He didn't say that he was worried about the depths of the channel. There hadn't been much rain lately, and if the water level had dropped too much, they were in trouble. Instead of voicing his concerns, he said, "I'll cast off."

As he strode to the back deck, he registered that Francesca was right. He was almost recovered from getting shot—thanks to recuperative powers of the werewolf constitution.

Outside, he found where she'd tied the lines to the branches above the boat.

When he'd freed the Lady Slipper from the unconventional mooring, he came back inside and started the engine. The gas gauge was pretty low, but he thought they had enough fuel to make it.

Francesca sat on the banquette near the pilot's chair, watching him move to the middle of the channel. He kept the speed low as he headed toward the other side of the swamp.

He had decided they were going to be okay when the boat struck a hidden obstruction below the surface and began making grinding noises as it struggled to move forward

"What happened?" Francesca asked, alarm in her voice.

"We're scraping the bottom," he answered as he backed up a little.

"The river's not deep enough for this boat?"

"Apparently." Changing course, he tried to steer toward the opposite bank, with little effect. The craft felt like it was trying to plow through liquid mud rather than water, and he knew he was going to damage the engine if he kept trying to batter his way through.

Instead, he reversed, easing away from the channel and heading toward the side again. But now the water was too low to maneuver.

Francesca gave him a worried look. "What are we going to do?"

"We're going to have to take the dinghy the rest of the way."

He looked back toward the cabins. "We'd better get what we need off the boat."

"How much can we carry?"

He laughed. "Only the essentials, like my laptop."

He brought the computer plus his equipment bag and gun then flooded the suitcase with their clothing and tossed it over the side. Next he set about getting the dinghy into the water. It was made of heavy-duty rubber, but detaching it from the Lady Slipper was hell on his arm. He positioned it off the end of the bigger boat before lowering the outboard into the water. At least he knew the craft would float, but he silently prayed the engine would start when he pulled the cord.

After stowing the laptop and equipment case inside a couple of large black garbage bags, he helped Francesca into the small craft. When she was settled in the bow, he lowered himself to the seat in the stern.

"Your arm's bleeding," Francesca said, as she gave him a quick inspection. We should have brought more bandages."

"We can do that later," he said, anxious to get to their destination.

To his relief, the small motor started, and they set off again, staying close to the right-hand bank. They were making good progress until he saw a lazy looking alligator sunning on a mud bank. He hoped it would stay there, but it raised its head, then slithered into the water and started toward them. Shit. What if the damn thing chomped the side of the rubber boat? They'd be in the water with nothing between them and the gator's jaws.

Francesca gasped.

He considered using his gun, but the sound of a shot would be like an alarm bell in the peaceful wildlife preserve.

His only option was to cut the engine, then reach for one of the oars lying on the boat's floor.

"What are we going to do?" Francesca gasped as the scaly body headed straight for the dinghy.

"Hang on tight."

She clenched her teeth and clutched the handles on the boat's sides as Zane stood and raised the oar. He slapped it in the water hoping that would warn the beast away, but it kept coming, probably thinking it had found an easy meal. When the creature drew close enough, Zane leaned over and whacked it on the top of its head as hard as he could with the sharp edge of the paddle. As the beast dove, the craft tipped dangerously.

Zane fell back onto the seat, scrambling not to fall out of the boat. Francesca reached to grab him, and they swayed together in the rocking craft.

Praying the alligator wasn't going to take another shot at them, Zane scanned the water. When he saw nothing but ripples, he breathed out a sigh of relief.

Starting the outboard again, he continued on course, this time keeping to the center of the waterway.

Francesca was on alert now, scanning one bank and then the

other. There were more gators sunning, but none of them stirred as the small boat passed.

They rounded a curve, and he saw what must be the marina up ahead. He'd told Francesca what to expect, but he wasn't exactly prepared for the knot of spectators being held back by police.

He glanced at his mate. "Get ready."

"Is this really okay?"

"Yes," he said, trying to sound like he meant it because his only option was to chug ahead, bouncing against a wooden dock as two cops with guns drawn rushed toward the dinghy.

Francesca looked like she'd rather be in a spaceship on the way to Mars than at this marina.

"It's going to be fine," he whispered, praying he had calculated this right.

18

"Out of the boat, and no funny stuff," a patrol officer ordered, his voice gruff as he threw Zane a line. He took it and tied up.

One of the uniforms helped Francesca out. Another man was keeping the crowd back from the scene of the capture.

"Okay folks. The excitement's over," he called out. But nobody was stepping back from the impromptu show. Zane could hear murmurs from the spectators and hoped none of them was going to do anything stupid.

"Hurry it up," another gruff voice advised him.

"Keep your shirt on," Zane snapped.

His arm was throbbing, but he made it to the dock under his own power. One of the cops climbed into the boat to pick up his bag with the computer. Two men on the reception committee pulled his and Francesca's hands behind their backs.

"Stop it," Francesca called out. "Can't you see his arm's bleeding?"

"He should have thought of that before he got himself into

trouble," one of the cops answered without breaking his stride. The officers marched them down the dock.

"Back up," another uniform shouted to the onlookers as the fugitives were escorted to a pair of waiting black and white Florida State Police cruisers. They were both helped into the back seat of the lead car. Two of the men climbed into another black and white and followed as they headed out of the marina.

Zane wanted to put his arm around Francesca and pull her close, but that was impossible.

The best he could do was mutter to their captors, "Nice performance. You can drop the Law and Order act now."

The driver turned to his prisoners with an apologetic expression on his face. "Sorry about the restraints. We had to make this look real. I'd stop and get the cuffs off of you, but I want to get out of the area before some hothead gets excited."

"You should have read us our rights," Zane answered after letting out the breath he'd been holding.

He looked from the driver to his life mate and back again. "Francesca, my brother Knox Marshall is driving. And the guy beside him is Jonah Raider. They're both Decorah agents—and good friends."

Francesca stared at them. "Are you both wolves?" she asked.

In the rearview mirror, Knox shot him a look. "I see you had to fess up to your lupine condition."

"It was either that or risk getting shot after she saw a wolf on the back deck of the boat."

"And why was a wolf there?"

"Chasing away a Florida panther."

Jonah cut into the conversation. "I'm not a wolf. I'm a telepath."

"A what?"

"Under the right circumstances, I can communicate mind to mind. It's useful for finding kidnap victims."

Francesca's head swung to Zane. "You didn't tell me about that."

"We don't talk about our talents unless we need to."

Knox gave him a smirk.

They headed for an airstrip where a small plane was standing by. The cars pulled up, and everybody got out. As promised, Jonah cut the wrist restraints off of Zane and Francesca.

Zane flexed his arm.

"You need a new bandage?" Knox asked.

Zane inspected his shirt. "It looks like it's stopped bleeding."

He and Francesca watched as the men opened the trunks of both cars, taking out equipment and going to work on the exteriors with some kind of cleaning solution. The white paint came off the top halves of the cars. The insignia and words "State Police" came off the bottom. The light bars on the top were also removed. When they were finished, two ordinary looking black cars sat at the side of the runway. All the equipment and cleaning supplies went into large plastic garbage bags which Jonah carried to the plane.

Francesca turned to the Decorah agents. "That was so real," she breathed. "For a few minutes I thought you really were cops."

"Didn't my brother tell you what was going to happen?" Knox said.

"Yes, but I couldn't picture it. And I couldn't help reacting."

"Well, that made it look real to the onlookers."

"How did you manage everything?" she asked, sounding like she still couldn't believe they'd actually pulled it off.

"Planning," Knox answered.

"Isn't all of this illegal? I mean impersonating cops. Taking away murder suspects."

"Yes. But we'll straighten it out later."

"You're sure nobody back at the marina is going to figure out you weren't the real thing?"

"If they do, we'll already be gone."

Luke Garner and Brand Marshall came over from the other car, and Zane introduced them.

Luke turned to Zane. "Why did you come in a small boat?"

"Because the Lady Slipper couldn't get through the channel. She's hung up a couple of miles from here."

"Okay. We'll tell the owner where to find it, and make sure he gets a bonus for retrieving it."

"Zane has a recording of his conversation with Tuckerman," Francesca said. "And you can hear the gunplay and his friend coming in."

"And accusing me of murder," Zane supplied.

"So the tape might be problematic," Jonah said.

"Then what are we going to do?" Francesca pressed.

"Hopefully, get enough evidence to figure out what's really going on. Luke's going to stay down here investigating."

"And I'm going to see if I can get any information from my father," Francesca added.

Zane nodded in agreement, then looked at Knox. "We're going directly to Newton?"

"Yeah."

His brother took off his uniform shirt. He was wearing a dark tee underneath. Stepping to the other side of the car, he changed from the trooper pants to jeans. The rest of the fake cops did the same, stuffing the uniform tops into another garbage bag.

While they waited for Brand to finish his preflight check, the men put the garbage bags in the cargo compartment. Then Zane, Francesca, Knox, and Jonah climbed into the passenger area. The plane was surprisingly roomy, with a dozen seats arranged in groupings facing each other across low tables.

When they had taken off, Francesca breathed out a sigh. "I can hardly believe we're really out of there. I know Florida is supposed to be a nice place to visit, but I'm never going back."

"Maybe in a few years," Zane said, then gave Francesca a concerned look. "You haven't had much to eat in the past few days."

"You either."

The other agents had brought steak for Zane, which he wolfed down raw, pardon the pun. Francesca sipped on a mug of beef and vegetable soup.

"Try to get some sleep," he told her.

"I don't think I can."

"Don't you think it's better if you're rested when we go to see your dad?" Zane asked.

"I guess you're right," she agreed.

The Decorah agents changed the configuration of the furniture, folding several of the chairs into beds, then drew a curtain across the cabin.

Francesca flopped onto one of the beds. Zane took the other. He was also sure he wasn't going to get any sleep, but fatigue and stress had taken their toll. He didn't wake up until Brand announced over the comms system that they would be landing in twenty minutes.

He blinked and looked out the window, seeing a large metro area below them. Glancing across at Francesca, he noted that her face was pinched. He reached out and squeezed her hand. "Everything's going to be okay."

"How can it be?"

"We'll make sure it is."

They landed at the small airport and taxied to the general aviation area, where a car was waiting. As soon as Francesca stepped off the plane, Zane saw her shiver.

"I forgot it was going to be cold up here," she said.

Knox came up behind her with a man's jacket. Wear this for now."

"Thanks."

Zane zeroed in on her expression. "Something else is bothering you."

"I want to get to my father as soon as possible. But I feel like a mess, and I must look like one, too."

"Why don't you call the nursing home, and see how he's doing. If you get a good report, we can stop on the way to clean up."

"Yes."

Zane pulled out the burner phone and handed it to Francesca. When she called the nursing home, they had some good news. Her father was better than when she'd left him.

Zane saw her face light up and slipped his arm around her shoulder.

"We'll be over in a couple of hours," she said, then looked at the Decorah agents for confirmation.

"Perfect," Knox said.

"Are you coming with us?" she asked.

"Yeah, for insurance."

She thought for a moment. "I could go home. I've got clothes there."

"But I don't," Zane countered. A little worm of worry gnawed at him.

"What does that expression mean?" Francesca demanded.

"I'd rather you not go home yet."

"Why?"

"Did your uncle know where you live?" he asked.

"No. I wasn't going to tell him until it seemed like everything was okay."

"Smart," Zane answered, but he was only partly reassured. He'd thought more than once that nothing about their present trouble was exactly as it seemed. He hoped her father's story would clear that up.

She clenched her teeth before relaxing her jaw. "Actually, I know now that my whole plan was a stupid idea."

"All you wanted to do was make your father happy."

"Yes, but it's too bad I didn't consult Decorah Security before I went charging down to Florida."

Zane answered with a small nod. She'd gotten herself into deep kimchi by contacting her uncle. And he couldn't help wondering if trouble had followed her north. But how?

"Why don't we repeat our Florida routine and stop at a discount department store."

She agreed and directed them to a shopping center where they both bought outfits suitable for the cooler Massachusetts weather. Then they drove to a chain motel not far from the nursing home.

Brand and Jonah waited in the car while Zane and Francesca checked in. When they were alone together, she stepped into his arms, and he clasped her tightly.

"My dad tends to get confused," she whispered. "What if he can't help figure how to get out of this fix?"

"Let's hope for the best," he answered, holding her for a few moments before easing away. "You go ahead and get dressed first."

"You're not going to shower with me?" she asked, obviously trying for a light tone.

"If I do, we're not getting out of here any time soon."

She squeezed his hand, then disappeared into the bathroom and closed the door.

He was pacing around the room when she came out, freshly showered and dressed and looking anxious again.

He showered and changed clothes in record time. When he came out, she was sitting at the table by the window, her head cupped in her hands.

"Let's do it," he said.

"I'm kind of afraid to go over there," she answered.

"Because?"

"Because I may not like what I'm going to hear."

"We'll deal with it."

"How—enter the Decorah Security fugitive protection program?"

"If we have to."

She clenched her fists before turning toward the door.

Outside, they slipped into the back seat of the car with the two waiting Decorah agents occupying the front.

"I've arranged for us to go in separate vehicles," Jonah said. "So it looks like you're alone."

"You think someone's watching the nursing home?" Francesca asked, an edge of tension in her voice.

"Not necessarily. But from what you've said, stuff keeps happening."

"You'll take this car after we pick up our vehicle," Jonah said.

Zane sat back and relaxed. From the sound of his friend's voice, he had something tricky in mind.

Jonah didn't disappoint. He drove to a strip mall a few miles from the motel where he and Knox went into a flower shop. When they returned they were wearing caps advertising Nelson Floral and holding a couple of flower arrangements.

"We were able to rent the shops delivery van for a few hours," Knox explained. "Perfect for a nursing home." He turned to Francesca. "You go in and talk to your father. We'll be lurking nearby. What's his room number?"

"Three twenty one, but the place is all on one floor, to make it easier for the residents. When you go in the front door, you walk all the way to the end of the hall and turn right. Then it's the . . ." she stopped and thought for a moment, "The fifth door on the left."

"Okay."

"But you can't just walk in there. You have to be making a delivery to a resident," Francesca said.

"We already thought of that. A generous donor has provided flower arrangements that everybody can enjoy in the dayroom."

"How far is the dayroom from your dad's room?" Zane asked.

"When you get to the end of the hall, you turn left instead of right. It's at the end of the corridor. But it's not that far."

"Got it," Jonah answered. He turned to Zane, "And let's arrange a little coordination before we split up."

The three Decorah agents huddled together for a few minutes. When they had agreed on a plan, the two bogus deliverymen walked to the van, where Knox opened the back door and set the flowers inside.

"You go ahead," Knox said. "We'll follow in a few minutes."

Zane slipped behind the wheel. Francesca took the passenger seat. Glancing over, he saw the grim set of her mouth. "It's going to be okay," he said gently, hoping he was telling the truth.

"I can't shake the feeling that I'm going to hear something that will change everything I know about my dad."

"You didn't think of that before you decided to visit your uncle in Florida?"

"Maybe a little. But I was so focused on making Dad happy by giving him back his brother. Then I went down there, and all my good intentions hit the fan."

"Yeah."

She kept her gaze on Zane. "And now I have to tell him that Uncle Angelo is dead."

"I know. I'm so sorry."

"It would have been better if I'd just left it alone."

"But then you wouldn't have met me."

She covered his hand with hers. "That's what makes all the bad stuff worth it."

He pulled into a space around the corner from the entrance.

"You were a regular visitor before you left for Florida?" he asked.

"Yes. They know me pretty well here."

When she started to get out, he put a hand on her arm. "Just let me look around first."

"I guess I'm not the only one who's jumpy."

"Just being cautious."

He stood on the sidewalk, sweeping his gaze over the parked cars and sniffing the air. He couldn't say exactly why, but he was uneasy.

When he saw motion from the corner of his eye, he turned and saw the flower truck pulling into a space at the front of the building. He didn't acknowledge the arrival of the other Decorah agents, but their presence was reassuring. Leaning in the passenger side window, he spoke to Francesca. "Let's get it over with."

She joined him on the sidewalk, but before she could approach the building, he put his hand on her arm to stop her.

"Do you ever bring visitors to see your father?" he asked.

"No."

"Then who am I? And if you're asked, why am I here with you?"

She didn't miss a beat. "To introduce my fiancé to my father." She looked over at him. 'That is, if wolves marry."

"God yes. But for now, I think it might work out better if nobody sees me."

"Why?"

"I'm not sure. But I can't ignore the hunch."

"There's a door at the end of the hall where Dad's room is located. I'll go in and open it."

"Thanks." He saw Francesca square her shoulders as she headed for the main entrance.

Zane took a narrow walkway along the side of the building and found the door he thought she meant. It had a large glass panel, and it was locked. After a few moments, he saw Francesca coming down the hall, heading for him.

She let him in, and they silently headed for room 301. As he passed, he saw bedrooms along the hall. All had hospital beds, some occupied by patients sleeping or watching television. But many were empty, and he supposed that most of the residents were in other parts of the facility engaging in various activities.

Francesca stopped at her father's room. When Zane looked in, he saw a frail man lying in bed. His hair was thin, his skin splotched, and the hand that lay on the covers was bony. He didn't stir, except that the hand twitched. Francesca crossed to him.

"Dad?"

At first he didn't respond.

"Dad?" she tried again.

His eyes blinked open, and he stared at his daughter, looking confused. "Rosa?"

"No, Dad. It's Francesca."

She pressed the button that raised the backrest before adjusting the pillow behind his head and leaning to kiss his forehead.

He kept his gaze on her, ignoring Zane. His voice was quavery as he said, "Francesca?"

"Yes."

He shook his head. "I thought you were my Rosa. This damn disease, it makes me see things that aren't there."

"I know. I'm sorry."

He switched topics abruptly. "Where have you been? I kept waiting for you."

"I needed to take a trip."

"Why didn't you tell me you were going away?"

She dragged in a breath and let it out. "I had to see how it turned out. I went to Florida to see your brother, Angelo."

As soon as she said the name, the old man gasped, alarm spreading across his features. "Angelo! I warned you. He's bad news."

She swallowed hard. "Yes. Something bad happened."

"It always does with him."

"Then why did you keep saying you wanted to see him?"

"Did I?"

She struggled to keep from shouting that she'd almost gotten killed because he'd wanted to see his brother. In an even voice, she said, "Yes you did. A lot. I thought it was important to you."

Her father's eyes pleaded for understanding. "I did want to see him—like he was when we were young. Then when we grew up, before he turned . . . bad. Selfish. Dangerous. He's the one who got me in trouble with the law. And I got in deeper and deeper, until I knew I had to escape."

She glanced helplessly at Zane, then turned back to her father as she covered the old man's hand with her own. "I guess he got himself into bad trouble. There's no easy way to say it. I'm afraid I have to tell you—he's dead."

"Oh my God. It was the mob, wasn't it?"

Francesca glanced at Zane again, then back at her father.

"I was at his house. We were talking and . . . rough-sounding men broke in. They killed him. And they went after me. I would have gotten killed if Zane hadn't saved me."

He had been standing a few feet away. When she ushered him forward, he approached the bed. Was she going to tell her father their relationship? Apparently she'd decided that was too much for now.

"Dad, Angelo's dead now. And the men who killed him went after me. You have to explain why. What was still wrong between you twenty years later?"

"I swore I'd never talk about it."

"But I'm still in danger. You have to give me more information."

His lips pressed into a grim line.

"Dad, I'm wanted by the police."

"Please, don't tell me that."

"But it's why you have to explain what happened between you and your brother. We need to figure out what's going on."

Francesca had been focused on them. Suddenly she was

aware of someone standing in the doorway. It was a short, slender man dressed in an expensive knit shirt and khaki pants. He had a medical mask over the lower half of his face, like he was afraid of getting an infection. His eyes were sharp and intense.

As Francesca watched, he pulled the mask down revealing thin lips curved into a grim smile. "She doesn't have to," he said to the man in the bed. "I will,"

Francesca's eyes bugged out when she saw his face and the gun he held in his hand.

"Uncle Angelo," she wheezed as she stared at the dead man. "But I heard those men kill you."

19

Angelo gestured with the gun, which Zane noted had a silencer.

"Move back toward the bed," he said, addressing both Zane and Francesca.

They moved. Zane could feel Francesca shaking beside him, and he put an arm around her waist.

"Steady."

To help her keep her balance, he clasped her against his side, thankful that the phone in his pocket was recording.

Fumbling behind himself, Angelo closed the door and tried to lock it, but there was no way for a patient to lock himself in. "You heard what I arranged for you to hear." He turned toward the man on the bed. "So you're Glen Turner now, you scumbag. All these years, I've been looking for you, and then sweet little Francesca calls and says you're dying. She says she wants us to kiss and make up. So I invite her down to my house in Naples."

He gave her a smug look. "I couldn't have planned it better if I had written the movie script."

"Those men who invaded your house were really working for you?" Zane qualified.

Angelo's expression turned nasty. "Yeah. And everything would have gone off without a hitch if you hadn't stuck your ugly mug in where it didn't belong."

"Why did you want me think you were dead?" Francesca blurted. "And why did you burn down your own house?"

"The place was a rental. No skin off my nose. And I wanted to be sure you'd cut and run."

"I could have gotten burned up."

"Naw. The guys started with a bunch of smoke—to make you think the house was burning. It got out of hand, but that was okay. You were always supposed to get away and run back here to your dipshit Daddy and tell him what had happened. I was gonna use that pendant to make sure that went as planned. I coulda had my men follow you to the airport and see where you were going, then had someone pick up your trail when you got home, but your boyfriend here screwed that up. So I thought about what to do and sent the guys to his house, but you got away." He glared at Zane. "I still had her fingerprints from the orange-juice glass. That was my backup—'cause I knew they'd be on record."

Zane gave him a questioning look. "Couldn't you just use the ID you found in her purse?"

Angelo glared at him. "I didn't know if it was legit. I mean, she and her dad have been hiding out for years. It could have been an elaborate hoax."

"You're the only one who's that tricky," the man in the bed muttered.

Zane was still after answers. "And you sent those men to kill us," he interjected.

Angelo laughed. "Well, to kill you. But not her. I still needed her to go running back to Daddy." He kept his focus on Zane.

"And you wouldn't give it up, would you? Why didn't you cut and run instead of trying to squeeze my guys?"

Zane didn't answer.

Francesca looked sick. "But why go to all that trouble to fake a murder scene? What's all this about?"

The intruder's gaze flicked toward his brother. "Back in the old days, your dad and I had a nice little hustle going until he got cold feet after the cops nabbed him." He spoke directly to the man on the bed. "I woulda gotten you out of it."

"Oh sure," Francesca's father answered.

Angelo ignored him and went on. "'You traded information for your hide, you rat. You got a lot of the guys sent to the slammer. Men who were loyal soldiers. I was lucky to get away, but not with my money. Where is it? What have you done with the cash you stole from me?"

Turner tried to push himself up, then collapsed back onto the bed.

"The money," his brother snarled.

"This is about money?" Francesca gasped.

Both brothers ignored her. A mixture of fear and defiance fought for dominance on the sick man's face. "I don't have it."

"What—you gave it to her?" He gestured toward Francesca.

"No!" the man who had become Glen Turner shouted. "It was dirty money. I didn't want anything to do with it. I gave it back to the people we stole it from."

Angelo's face reddened, and he let loose with a string of curses. "You stupid son of a bitch. All this plotting and planning for nothing. One of my best guys is dead. Another's in the hospital, and two are chewed up by a dog. I was gonna make you pay for screwing me out of my money—and have your daughter watch. Now you'll all pay."

Zane fought not to look toward the door. Christ, where were Jonah and Knox? This would be a good time for them to arrive.

He knew he was listening to the ranting of a psychopath.

And once again he was thinking he had no other choice about how to keep the guy from killing everyone in the room. Moving slowly, he inched away from Francesca. Under his breath, he had begun to say the chant of transformation.

"*Taranis, Epona, Cerridwen,*" he murmured, then repeated the same phrase and went on to another set of ancient words.

Francesca heard and gave him a startled glance, but she must have understood what he was doing because he'd told her she wouldn't hear that chant again unless she was going to see a wolf.

"*Ga. Feart. Cleas. Duais. Aithriocht. Go gcumhdai is dtreorai na deithe thu.*"

He felt his jaw elongate, his teeth sharpen, his body contort as muscles and limbs transformed themselves into a different shape. He hadn't been able to get rid of his clothes, but his pants slipped off and his shirt flapped around him as he leaped forward.

Angelo was paralyzed in front of him, as he watched something that had to be impossible taking place before his eyes.

Then he screamed, found he could move, and raised the gun.

But the man who had been standing beside the bed was gone, and the bullet smashed into the wall across the room at the same time the door burst open. Angelo whirled and fired again, but another wolf came in low, taking him down, clamping fangs onto his neck and dragging him into the hall.

There were running feet in the corridor now and people screaming. The two wolves dashed for the back of the building where Zane had come in. They pushed the doors open with their momentum as they disappeared from view.

Francesca knew she had to act quickly. Stooping down, she scooped up Zane's pants and shoved them into one of the drawers where her father's clothing was stored.

She was just in time. Again there was a scream in the hall, and a nurse rushed into the room.

"Are you all right?" the woman gasped out.

"Yes. What happened?"

"I . . . I don't know."

The nurse was partially blocking Francesca's view. Peering around her, she saw Angelo sprawled on the tile floor of the hall, a pool of blood around his head and neck.

"Stay in your room," the nurse said. "We're on lockdown until that animal is caught."

Caught? She prayed the wolves had gotten away.

As the woman closed the door, Francesca hurried back to her father. He was lying in the bed shaking, mumbling to himself.

"Dad, are you all right?"

"I don't know. I must have had another one of those damned hallucinations."

"Yes, right," she soothed.

He gave her a dazed look. "Was Angelo here? Did I make him up?"

Deciding honesty was best, she answered, "He was here."

Turner shook his head. "My own brother. He came to kill me. I knew he had turned rotten. I can't believe he would go that far."

"It's over now," Francesca soothed, but her father kept talking.

"He said I took his money. But it wasn't his money. He stole it."

"Yes. I'm sorry." She swallowed hard. "This is my fault."

"No!"

"Yes. He never would have found you, but I got in touch with him and went down to Florida because you kept saying that you wanted to see him."

The old man's face contorted. "I did, and I didn't. I wanted to make things right with him. But I now I know that would have been impossible. All he wanted was to get that money back —and to punish me for taking it away."

She pressed her hand over his. "But it's all over now. He can't hurt you. He's dead."

"How?"

She gulped. "It was like a freak accident. A large animal was in the nursing home. It got him."

"But how?"

"There must have been a vicious dog on the loose," she answered lamely, wondering if Dad was going to point out there were two dogs. But maybe he had blended them into one.

Her father seemed to buy into her explanation—probably because he wanted to. But would the police believe the story?

"Where did your young man go? Or did I make him up, too?"

"He went to get the police," Francesca answered, knowing they were going to show up soon. "But it's best if you don't tell them he was here."

He studied her tense expression. "All right."

In the distance she could hear sirens blaring.

Suddenly exhausted, she sat down in the chair beside the bed. Where was Zane? She wanted him to come back, but she understood why she had to carry this off alone. Forcing herself not to grip the wooden arms, she folded her hands in her lap.

She could hear voices in the hall. Finally when a uniformed officer opened the door and strode into the room, she felt tension crackling through her body. Would this guy realize she was the woman who was wanted for murder in Naples, Florida?

Playing the part of a terrified bystander, she asked, "Is it safe to come out now?"

"The building is clear."

"Thank God."

The cop had a notebook in his hand. His name tag said, "Murphy."

"You're." He looked at his notepad. "Mr. Turner's daughter, Francesca?"

"Yes. I was visiting him."

"Did you see anything?" he asked.

"Well, a nurse came in, and I saw . . . a man on the floor. Is he all right?"

"Do you know him?"

This was it—the jackpot question. While she was still deciding how to answer, two more men entered the room. Her heart leaped when she saw one of them was Zane. The other was an older man she didn't know. He spoke to the cop.

"I'm Frank Decorah, head of the Decorah Security Agency, and this is one of my agents, Zane Marshall. He was on assignment in Florida when he got involved in a murder investigation."

An interesting way to put it, Francesca thought. Zane was fully dressed, and she had to figure the guys in the flower truck had brought clothing for him.

Decorah gestured toward Francesca. "The dead man is her uncle. Before he died, he admitted coming here to murder her father and her, too. We have that confession on tape as well as his admission that he sent thugs to murder Ms. Turner and my associate." He didn't add that his operative and Ms. Turner were murder suspects down south.

The cop stared at him. "A confession on tape?"

"Yes. We need to go over to your station house where Ms. Turner and Mr. Marshall can give a statement and turn over the tapes."

"But what happened to the dead man? How did he get mauled by a large animal—or two large animals inside this nursing facility?"

"No idea," Frank Decorah said. "You can stay here to continue that investigation, or you can escort us to the station house."

"I don't appreciate a member of the public dictating police actions," Murphy snapped.

"Of course," the Decorah chief said. "Which is why you may want to contact your lieutenant. I have further pertinent information relevant to the investigation."

"What?" the cop demanded.

"I'd rather keep it private, which is why we should go to the station."

While Frank was talking to the officer, Zane moved to stand beside Francesca's chair. When he reached for her hand, she turned her palm up and gripped his fingers.

"Are you okay?" he murmured.

"Mostly. What about you?"

"I'm fine."

Murphy was speaking to someone on the phone now.

Keeping her voice low, Francesca asked Zane, "You had your phone recorder on when you came in here?"

"Yes."

"But your phone is still in your pants pocket."

"I was transmitting it to Knox and Jonah."

"Oh. Good thinking."

"And I see you got rid of my pants."

"In one of the drawers."

Murphy interrupted their conversation. "We're all going down to the station." He made it sound like he was the one issuing a decree.

He looked at Zane and Francesca. "You're riding in a police cruiser."

"Of course," Zane said.

They were ushered into the back, with a different officer driving, but at least they weren't handcuffed. Frank Decorah trailed in his rental.

"When did your boss get here?" Francesca asked.

"Just after the excitement in the nursing home." He looked

from her to the cop driving the cruiser, and she nodded and stopped talking.

When they arrived, they were ushered into an interrogation room, where they waited for several minutes for a lieutenant to appear. Again, Zane made it clear from his body language that it was better not to talk while they were alone.

The door finally opened, and a broad-shouldered man in a suit strode into the room. He looked to be in his mid-forties, with strands of gray creeping into his dark hair.

"I'm Lieutenant Henderson," he said. His next words were, "I'd like to hear why you think you shouldn't be arrested for murder."

20

Francesca felt an electric sizzle go through her.

Beside her, Zane spoke calmly. "That will be clear when I explain what happened after thugs burned down Angelo Lucci's house. Francesca can tell you what happened before that—before I found her running for her life down the beach."

He turned to Francesca. "Why don't you start?"

She told the story of contacting her uncle, coming to Florida, and thinking he had been murdered. She also related what she'd heard when she was hiding in the closet and how she'd escaped from the burning house.

Then Zane took up the narrative, methodically, going through the events of the previous two days, noting where he had documentary evidence to back up his story—including pictures of the men who followed them from his rental. He also produced the pendant which had hidden the tracking device and finished with, "Frank Decorah assures me that the Lady Slipper has been returned to the Cypress Creek marina."

The lieutenant said, "That sounded pretty glib. But I've been in touch with the authorities in Naples. What do you have to say about Decorah Security men impersonating police officers?"

Francesca winced and Zane answered the question.

"The only way we could prove our innocence was to stay out of custody so we could get the full story from Francesca's father."

"A lawyer could have done that," Henderson said.

Francesca interjected, "He would have been reluctant to speak to a lawyer. He was in the Federal Witness Protection Program and very wary of revealing anything about himself."

"You have proof that his brother came to kill him?" Henderson pressed.

"Yes. Zane recorded him in the hospital room threatening her and her father."

"It was pretty convenient that he was killed before he could shoot anybody," the lieutenant said.

Francesca answered. "He tried. There are bullet holes in the walls of the room. I assume the bullets will match the gun he was carrying."

"What stopped him?" Henderson asked.

"The dogs burst in."

"And where did *they* come from?"

Francesca shook her head. "I don't know anything about them. I certainly didn't bring them with me."

Henderson scowled. "Another interesting convenience," he muttered.

He kept questioning them, but he couldn't shake the story that they had been defending themselves during the whole Florida episode.

Finally, he said, "You will have to remain in the area until this is cleared up."

"Of course," Zane agreed before fixing his gaze on the lieutenant. "But there's one more consideration."

Henderson waited for him to elaborate.

"We know Mr. Turner's brother, Angelo Lucci, came up here to kill him. We know he was running a con on Francesca in Florida. He's dead, but there were several men who pursued us after she escaped from his house. If they were working for Lucci, then I hope we're out of danger because their boss is dead. If they're holding a grudge, then they may come here looking for us. Or they might come after Mr. Turner in the nursing home."

Francesca's head swung toward him. "I didn't think of any of that," she whispered.

"Those are fair points," Henderson agreed. If everything you've told me is true," he added.

"Do you have any suggestions for insuring our safety while we hang around town?" Zane asked.

The lieutenant thought it over. "I suggest that Ms. Turner not go back to her apartment. We can put you in a hotel we use for witnesses."

"And since I know it would be a strain on your department to guard Mr. Turner twenty-four seven, I think Decorah Security can keep watch over him," Zane added.

"All right," Henderson agreed. He looked at Francesca, "And I believe it would be safer if you stay away from your father until the whole matter is resolved. If the wrong people are hanging around, they could follow you back to the hotel."

She felt her chest tighten. "He's old and very sick. I . . ."

Before she could finish, Zane cut in. "We need to determine that the nursing home isn't being watched. If nobody shows up after a few days, it should be all right to go over there." He turned back to Henderson. "And I think Frank Decorah has made hotel arrangements for us. If you agree to the location." He gave Henderson the address. The hotel was okay with the lieutenant, and Zane and Francesca finally left.

When they were out on the street, she looked at him. "Where are we staying?"

"A boutique hotel that's not far from here."

Knox was waiting for them down the street and called Zane on his cell phone when they reached the sidewalk. He was also staying at the same hotel. On the way over, Zane filled him in on what had happened in the interview, with Frank listening in on the phone.

The hotel was in a charming Victorian mansion that had been beautifully restored. Zane and Francesca had a large room decorated in soft beige and rose. In addition to the bed, there was a small sitting area with a couch and chair.

Francesca turned to Zane. "I keep feeling like every time we reach a safe place, something else happens."

"This time, it's going to turn out okay."

"How can you be so sure?"

"Because things are falling our way." He gave her a reassuring kiss. "You get some rest. I'm going to talk to the other Decorah agents."

Francesca turned back the damask spread on the bed, kicked off her shoes, and lay down with the rest of her clothes on. The day had started in Florida getting stuck in the swamp and ended in Massachusetts with her uncle coming back from the dead like an evil jack-in-the-box. Only, surprise, he had never been dead. That had all been an elaborate hoax.

She closed her eyes and didn't open them again until Zane came back into the room. She looked up to see he was carrying a tray.

"What time is it?" she asked, fighting for coherence.

"After ten."

"I slept that long?"

"Yes, you needed it."

Zane set down the tray on the coffee table in front of the sofa.

Francesca came over to the sitting area. When she lifted the cloth covering, she found a cardboard container of chicken soup.

"I figured you liked it," he said. "We had it brought in from a restaurant down the street."

"Thank you."

He sat down beside her as she spooned up some soup. When she was almost finished, he said, "I have some news."

He saw her tense and slung his arm around her shoulder. "It's good news. The guy you hit, whose name is Fritz Eldridge, is recovering nicely. At first he wouldn't say anything about the case. Then the cops informed him that he doesn't have to be afraid of Angelo Lucci because he's dead. There was an armed robbery warrant out on Eldridge. They said he could get a better deal if he cooperated. He thought that over for a few minutes and started confirming our story about what happened at your uncle's house. It was a scam to lead Angelo to your dad, so he could kill him. He also confirmed that Conrad shot me before I shot him. And one more thing. He also told the cops where to find the other three men who were involved in the plot."

Her throat was so tight she could barely get the words out to ask, "And what about my hitting him over the head?"

"He said it stopped him from killing me."

She breathed out a sigh of relief but had one more question. "There's still the problem of our breaking into their house."

"That was a little trickier to get around, since technically we should never have been in there. But Frank Decorah got a very good lawyer who argued that we were only trying to find out why they were hunting us down."

She gave him a wondering look. "Then it's really over?"

"Yes."

"Oh Lord, I . . . I couldn't let myself believe it was really going to be okay."

He turned her toward him. "I know."

"How?"

"You were so tight and closed up."

"I'm sorry. I was still afraid we would lose each other."

He pulled her close, rocking her in his arms. "Never. I guess I coped with it differently. I started making plans for the future. And now I need to know if they work for you—or if you feel like I've overstepped."

"I'd like to hear what you were thinking."

"That since you do freelance editing, you could do it in Maryland."

She considered that for a moment. "Yes. A lot of my clients can work by e-mail, although I'll probably have to look for some new ones. But what about my dad?"

"We can move him down there too. The IT guys have been scouting nursing homes near Decorah headquarters. There are a couple that look really good. Or I have another suggestion."

She tipped her head to the side. "Like what?"

"It's a long story, but Decorah has a special program for brain-damaged patients. It started when we took over a research project on men and women who were in comas. The project hooks them up to a virtual reality system that allows them to lead normal lives."

"I don't understand."

"It's a little hard to explain. I guess it's like being inside a video game where everything seems perfectly like reality. The people there are 'living' in a luxury hotel with every amenity. If your dad joined them, his body would be asleep, but his mind and virtual body would be in a world where he could be like his old self. Doing all the things he used to enjoy before he got sick. We can talk to Lily Wardman, the director. Her sister lives there. And one of our agents, her husband Mack spent a lot of time in the facility. He was a fighter pilot. His plane crashed, and the doctor who was running the experiment illegally added him to the project. That's how Decorah got involved. We can visit the place, and you and your dad can decide if it's right for him."

"It sounds too good to be true."

"Yeah. That's why we'll make sure it's the right fit." He gave her a long look. "I hope you don't think I'm pushing anything on you."

"No. I like that you're thinking about him."

"And us," he added.

"Yes." She hesitated before asking, "Did anyone ever tell you you make a very handsome wolf?"

He laughed. "You don't think my brothers and my cousins are going to say *that* do you?"

"Your mom?"

His expression turned serious. She never talked about that, either."

"Why not?"

"I think if she'd had her choice, she would have wanted her boys to be 'normal.'"

"Sorry."

"It's what it is." He switched subjects abruptly. "I hope you're going to like my house. It isn't large, but I've got a lot of land. It's on the edge of a regional park. And you can have fun making my bachelor pad into a home."

"I'd love to. And I understand that a wolf needs space to run —and hunt."

She paused for a moment, then said in a rush, "With my dad in Witness Protection, I wondered if I could find the right man to marry. Someone who wouldn't care about my background and someone who could keep it a secret. I found the perfect guy when you snagged me running up the beach."

He made a low sound. "You better believe that a wolf wonders how he's going to discover the right mate. But against all odds, we found each other."

"Yes."

"You're going to love the Decorah community. You've already met some of the agents. And the wives are all friends." He laughed, "The guys have probably been taking bets on when I was going to find a life mate."

"Why?"

"Because they could see I was restless. That's why I took an assignment in Florida. Plus my younger brother, Knox, had already found a mate."

"Thank God you did." She gave him an anxious look. "You think I'll fit in?"

"I know you will. But right now how about we celebrate coming through a pretty harrowing experience?"

She loved the sudden wolfish look in his eye. When he reached for her, she clasped her hands around the back of his head and brought his mouth to hers. The kiss was long and deep. A sign of their commitment and a promise for the future.

- The End -

AFTERWORD

Thank you for purchasing *Fire on the Moon*. I hope you enjoyed reading it as much as I loved writing it.

If you enjoy my books, do me a huge favor. Please go back to your favorite online bookstore, and leave an honest review. Authors live and die by their reviews. The few extra seconds it takes are really appreciated. Thank you!

If you'd like to learn more about Mack Bradley and Lily Wardman, you'll find an excerpt from their story, *Rx Missing*, at the end of this book.

ALSO BY REBECCA YORK

If you enjoy *Fire on the Moon,* you might also like to read other Light Street Press books by Rebecca York:

DECORAH SECURITY SERIES

Book 1. **On Edge** (a Decorah Security prequel novella)

Book 2. **Dark Moon** (a novel)

Book 3. **Chained** (a novella)

Book 4. **Ambushed** (a short story)

Book 5. **Dark Powers** (a novel)

Book 6. **Hot and Dangerous** (a short story)

Book 7. **At Risk** (a novel)

Book 8. **Christmas Captive** (a novella)

Book 9. **Destination Wedding** (a novella)

Book 10. **Rx Missing (**a novel)

Book 11. **Hunting Moon** (a novel)

Book 12 **Terror Mansion** (a novella)

Book 13. **Outlaw Justice** (a novella)

Book 14. **Found Missing** (a novel)

Book 15. **Preying Game** (a novel)

Book 16. **Boxed In** (a novel)

Book 17. **Hollow Moon** (a novella)

Book 18. **Can She Get Home for Christmas?** (a novella)

Decorah Security Collection (includes Ambushed, Hot and Dangerous, and Dark Powers)

And if you like science-fiction romance, you might enjoy the following Rebecca York books:

OFF WORLD SERIES

Book 1. **Hero's Welcome** (an off-world series short story)

Book 2. **Nightfall** (an off-world series novella)

Book 3. **Conquest** (an off-world series short story)

Book 4. **Assignment Danger** (an off-world novella)

Book 5. **Christmas Home** (an off-world short story)

Book 6. **Firelight Confession** (an off-world novella)

Off-World Collection (includes Nightfall, Hero's Welcome, and Conquest)

PRAISE AND AWARDS

* *New York Times* and *USA Today* best-selling Author
* Two-time Rita finalist in the prestigious RWA writing contest
* Recipient of two *RT Book Reviews* Career Achievement Awards
* Recipient of the RWA Centennial Award
* Prism Award winner
* *Affaire de Coeur* Critics Choice Award for Contemporary Novel

"Rebecca York delivers page-turning suspense." -Nora Roberts

"Rebecca York will thrill you with romance, kill you with danger and chill you with the supernatural." -Patricia Rosemoor

"Rebecca York's writing is fast-paced, suspenseful, and loaded with tension." -Jayne Ann Krentz

ABOUT THE AUTHOR

A *New York Times* and *USA Today* Best-Selling Author, Rebecca York is a 2011 recipient of the Romance Writers of America Centennial Award. Her career has focused on romantic suspense, often with paranormal elements.

Her 16 Berkley books and novellas include her nine-book werewolf "Moon" series. *Killing Moon* was a launch book for the Berkley Sensation imprint. She has written for Harlequin, Berkley, Dell, Tor, Carina Press, Silhouette, Kensington, Running Press, Tudor, Pageant Books, and Scholastic.

Her many awards include two Rita finalist books. She has two Career Achievement awards from Romantic Times: for Series Romantic Suspense and for Series Romantic Mystery. And her Peregrine Connection series won a Lifetime Achievement Award for Romantic Suspense Series.

Many of her novels have been nominated for or won RT Reviewers Choice awards. In addition, she has won a Prism Award, several New Jersey Romance Writers Golden Leaf awards and numerous other awards, and she is on the Romance Writers of America Honor Roll.

CONTACTS

Rebecca York loves to hear from readers!

Website: http://www.rebeccayork.com
Email: rebecca@rebeccayork.com
Twitter: @rebeccayork43
Facebook: http://www.facebook.com/ruthglick
Blog: http://www.rebeccayork.blogspot.com

Sign up for Rebecca York's **Newsletter**
to get all the scoop on Rebecca's
SEXY ROMANTIC SUSPENSE at:
http://rebeccayork.com/newsletter

EXCERPT OF RX MISSING

BY REBECCA YORK

PROLOGUE

From his F18 fighter jet, Lieutenant Commander Mack Bradley looked down on a scene of destruction.

His chest tightened as he listened to the choppy, breathless voice of a man trapped in his disabled Humvee.

"This is Whiskey Two Romeo. Convoy hit by roadside bomb. Rockets. Automatic weapons. Repeat Whiskey Two Romeo. The bastards are in the hills to our left. . . Sweet Jesus . . . can you lay down fire . . .?"

Mack kept his own emotions in check as he came around to the convoy's position.

Stay cool. Do your job. Then get the hell out.

When he got the all clear, he executed the attack, diving on the enemy, delivering a series of 500 pounders before zooming upward again. A typical Middle Eastern bombing run, he thought with satisfaction as he headed back toward the carrier.

Only this time, a heat-seeking missile zeroed in on his engine. He felt the teeth-rattling impact, saw the fire warning light and knew he had only two choices. Go down with the plane or eject.

No choice at all, really, because the escape procedures had been drilled into him.

Adrenaline surged through his system, as he began sending out his call sign and location. There was no time for fear or worry. He simply acted automatically.

"Mayday, Mayday, Mayday. This is Lightning 22 ejecting twenty miles south of Senadar. Repeat this is Lightning 22."

No response came in the moments he had left in the crippled aircraft. He had to trust that they'd heard him as he pulled the handle on the seat between his legs, got his body into position, and prayed that the chute would open.

Seconds later, the seat blasted out of the cockpit with a force of 17 Gs.

As he tumbled through space, there was nothing more to do but wonder if he was going to live or die.

Then, like the old clichéd phrase, his entire life flashed through his mind. He smiled as he tasted his mom's chocolate chip cookies. Felt again the joy and pride of catching the winning touchdown in the Allegheny County championship game. The scenes came fast and furious, each with the emotions of the moments he'd spent on earth. Hunting expeditions with his dad and twin brother. Midshipman at Annapolis. Flight training. The wild bachelor party before his disastrous marriage.

The sum total of his life. He'd thought he had years to enjoy it, but it had turned out to be so damn short.

He tried to grab on to a good memory—like back when he and Grant had always known what the other was thinking. Instead he had a few stabbing moments to remember how he and Gail had hurt each other. Then everything went black.

CHAPTER ONE

At one in the morning, the Winston Funeral Home was quiet as a tomb. The back door had been locked, but Grant Bradley had learned long ago how to get in and out of the right and wrong places.

After slipping his lock picks back into his knapsack, he quietly closed the door and stood for a moment in the dimly lit hallway, listening for signs that he'd been discovered.

But no one dead or alive challenged him. If a rent-a-cop appeared, he could always say that grief made men do strange things.

He'd seen that as a CIA agent. Experienced it for himself when he'd abandoned a promising career as a spook to come home and stare into space until Frank Decorah had asked him to join Decorah Security. That hadn't worked out so well either. Not when he'd compared his talents to the other guys in the agency. They had several werewolves on staff and a guy who picked up memories from objects he touched. Grant had felt like a second-class member of the team. So he'd left after a couple of years—over Frank's objections. Frank had said Grant's talents were going to blossom, but he'd seen no evidence of it. And when Dad had gotten too old to handle his Western Maryland outfitter business, Grant had come home to take it over.

He'd asked Mack to join him. The Bradley twins working as a team again, but his five-minutes-older sibling was still flying high as a Navy pilot, and look where it had gotten him.

Mack was in one of the reception rooms. His body was supposed to be pretty beaten up, which was why the casket lid had been screwed down tight.

But that wasn't going to stop Grant from saying good-bye —his way.

He'd coped with the grief of his and Mack's friends all day, plus the awkward encounter with his brother's ex-wife.

Now he was alone. Very alone. As kids, he and Mack had gotten inside each other's minds. That talent had faded when they'd matured. But not his love for his brother.

A man with a mission, he moved stealthily toward the coffin which sat on a velvet-draped table. He wasn't going to break down. He was just going to pay his final respects to a man he had loved with an unwavering steadiness, even when they'd had their disagreements.

As he rested his hand on the polished mahogany of the coffin top, he spoke quiet words to his brother—his best friend.

"I've missed you, Mackie. Sorry you didn't get home for Christmas this year. And that we didn't get a chance to do some fishing in the fall." He dragged in a breath and went on, struggling to hold his voice steady.

"Remember the fun times we had together? On the football team. At Ocean City after our senior year. And remember that fight with the Frostburg guys in back of the bowling alley where we got busted by the cops, and Dad had to bail us out. He was mad as hell, and we had to chop wood for the entire winter to make up for that one."

He knew he was stalling because he didn't want to look

inside the coffin. Yet he *had to*. Was that a little bit of the old psychic ability coming back to him? He scoffed at the rationalization and kept talking.

"I brought you some stuff that you might like to have. That championship football that you kept in your room. Your high school ring. And a Snickers bar. Your favorite."

Grant rummaged in the knapsack again for a Phillips screwdriver, then went to work on the screws that held the lid down.

He carefully set them on the velvet-topped table before closing his eyes for a moment and saying a prayer for strength.

Steeling himself, he lifted the lid with a jerk and looked down into the coffin. A gasp escaped his lips as he struggled to understand the horror of what he was seeing.

Mack's body was not in the coffin.

Not Mack or anybody else.

Nestled in the silk padding was a featureless man-sized prosthetic *thing* in place of his brother's remains. Like a department store dummy, only it must have been a lot heavier, since it had to make up the mass of a physically fit, full-grown man.

Emotions smashed through Grant in quick succession like interior shotgun blasts as he struggled to come to grips with the implications.

Shock. Then relief. Then a hundred questions. Was his brother alive—and somewhere else? And if so, where?

That was followed by worry and fear. If he was alive, what had happened to him?

In the end, Grant was left with stone-cold fury as he pulled out his cell phone and took a picture of the lifeless hulk that mocked him in the coffin. Hardly able to keep his hand steady, he mailed the picture to his computer, then to cloud storage.

What the hell was going on here, and where was his brother?

If Mack wasn't at the Winston Funeral Home, where the hell was he? And why?

He lowered the lid of the coffin but didn't bother screwing it down, then closed his eyes, feeling like a fool yet desperate enough to try the old trick he and his twin had shared.

"Mack," he whispered. "Can you hear me Mack?" He kept projecting the message, but there was no answer, and finally he gave up.

Well, gave up on the attempt at mental contact—but not on finding out why his brother's supposedly mangled body had been replaced by a faceless dummy.

CHAPTER TWO

The moment Mack Bradley woke, he knew something was very wrong. At first it was just a kind of free-floating anxiety. A dread he couldn't identify. But it soon solidified into a more concrete apprehension that sent a shudder skittering over his skin.

Lying very still, he stared at the open wooden-railed canopy above the wide, soft bed. Cautiously he sat up for a better view of the room and saw a writing desk in some English antique style he couldn't name and a hallway leading to a marble bathroom. Across from the bed was a long, inlaid dresser with a flat-screen TV.

He threw back the covers, swung his legs out of the bed, and noted that he was wearing a navy blue warm-up suit with a white tee shirt under the jacket.

Feeling a little unsteady on his feet, he kept one hand on the bed as he dug his toes into the thick Oriental carpet.

He was in what looked like a very expensive five-star hotel room, not that he'd spent a lot of time in luxury digs.

But he could be on leave. Maybe Dubai or Bangkok? He'd

enjoyed R and R in both those locations and splurged on deluxe accommodations. This was the kind of room he'd expect there.

Had he gotten drunk out of his mind last night? And ended up here alone?

Possibly, except that he didn't remember checking into any hotels. Or dressing in the warm-up suit.

The memory gap made his chest tighten painfully. Wracking his brain, he tried to dredge up the last thing he remembered. From somewhere in the stratosphere, it zinged back to him with gut-churning force.

He'd just dropped a couple of five hundred pounders on some murderous insurgents when a missile had come whistling up his ass.

Now he was *here*.

Or was the mission all a nightmare?

No. He remembered dropping the bombs. Remembered the crippled plane. All that was real. Not like this place.

His stomach clenched. Where was he *exactly?*

Heaven? Hell? A hospital?

Was he dead or alive?

Or what?

He balled his hands into fists, digging his nails into his palms, struggling to ground himself.

He had vague memories of another bed. Narrow. With high sides. A woman taking care of him, speaking to him in a soothing voice, telling him he was safe now. That everything was going to be okay.

He'd opened his eyes and looked at her. Struggled to answer her, but he hadn't been able to get any words out. Now the scene skittered out of reach. Had *that* just been a dream?

No. Like the bombing raid, it felt real.

"Calm down," he muttered aloud partly to hear the sound of his own voice. "You'll figure this out."

He flexed his arms and legs, feeling the muscles work, reassured by the physical sensations. Pulling up his tee shirt, he looked down at his abdomen and chest. No injuries as far as he could tell.

Which was good. Right?

In the bathroom, he switched on the light and saw a huge soaking tub, a separate glassed-in shower, a black granite vanity with double bowls and a separate little room for the toilet.

A razor, shaving cream, deodorant, toothbrush and toothpaste were neatly lined up on the shelf above the sink.

The toothpaste tube was new. So he'd just gotten here, right? Which was why he didn't remember this place.

But shit, he must have checked in. And he didn't recall that at all.

He stared at himself in the mirror. Dark hair. Dark eyes. The scar on his chin from when he'd fallen out of a tree when he was eight. He'd been dazed, and Grant had helped him back to the house.

Relief washed over him that he recognized the man who stared back.

But where the hell was he?

His heart began to pound as hard as it had been pounding when he'd pulled the ejection lever on his seat and blasted out into the naked sky. What if ISIS had scooped him up after he'd bailed out?

And then what? They sure as hell wouldn't have installed him in this palace. Instead he'd be in a dark, dank cell with cockroaches for companions. Not a luxury hotel. Unless they were trying something very tricky? Like that TV series where they convert the guy to Islam.

He was about to fill the glass from the tap to moisten his dry mouth when he saw a bottle of water on the sink. Maybe he'd better use that.

After taking a drink, he said his name aloud.

"Mack Bradley. Lieutenant Commander, US Navy. Born and

raised in Cumberland, Maryland. Cumberland High School. Naval Academy. Divorced."

That last part hurt. He'd been in the Gulf when Ginny had written him to say she couldn't take the long absences anymore, and she was moving on with her life, with a guy she'd met at work, it turned out.

He rubbed his hand against his chin. No beard stubble. But he didn't remember shaving.

Repressing a curse, he walked into the dressing area and looked at the neatly hanging clothes, everything from jeans and tee shirts to more dressy sports clothes. Curious about the size, he took down a pair of well-washed jeans. They fit comfortably, and he folded the sweatpants onto the hanger before pulling on a black tee shirt, then a pair of running shoes and socks that were also his size.

Once he was dressed, he looked toward the wall of drapes in the bedroom. When he thought about pulling them aside and taking a look at his surroundings, his stomach clenched into a tight, hot knot. "Jesus. What do you think?" he muttered to himself since he was the only person here. "That you're going to see smoking pools of brimstone?"

Or maybe a psychiatrist on the balcony who would explain that he was in a high class mental hospital, and he wasn't getting out any time soon.

Teeth clenched, he pulled the heavy fabric aside and peered out onto a lush green lawn bordered by beds of tropical foliage. Magenta bougainvillea climbed up a high stucco wall bordering a forest. From his vantage point, it seemed that he was on the second floor of a two-story building. Perpendicular to his room, he saw another wing of the hotel.

The peaceful scene was reassuring, until he noticed that nothing was moving out there. Not a person. Not a bird. Not an insect.

When he snatched up the phone on the bedside table, he

heard no dial tone. But there had to be someone at the desk downstairs. Someone who could tell him where he was. Except that he was going to feel like an idiot getting into that kind of conversation. Perhaps it was better to play it cool, scout around, and see what he could find out.

Before exiting the bedroom, he looked toward the television set. There was a remote lying under it, and he picked it up and pressed the power button. He got a menu with movies, games, TV. There was a large selection of all three, but he found no live television—only prerecorded shows. If he was bored, he could watch some of this stuff, but he wanted reality, not canned programing.

He turned off the set again and walked down a short hall into a living room furnished in the same opulent style as the bedroom. His keycard was in a slot by the door.

The plastic rectangle had a red and gold design of scrollwork and arches that looked vaguely Middle Eastern—or Indian—but there was no hotel name.

After pocketing the card, he stepped into the hall. No brimstone. Only a long runner of Oriental carpet over polished wood at the sides of the hall, and striped paper on the walls.

He was in room 222.

After noting the number, he hurried to a wide marble staircase which led to a lobby furnished with groups of comfortable couches and chairs.

All very tasteful and very expensive. A stage set with no people.

And when he tried to turn on a computer on the check-in desk, nothing happened.

He thought about cupping his hand around his mouth and calling out, "Anybody here?" Or maybe, "where the hell is everybody?"

But that could be dangerous.

Christ, what if terrorists had taken over the hotel? They'd

killed everybody in sight, and they were waiting for the next victim to show up.

But if they'd done it, the attack had been totally silent. Besides, he saw no bodies. No blood. No signs of a struggle like overturned chairs and tables or broken knickknacks on the floor.

He was heading across the lobby when a muffled scream made him stop and reverse directions.

- End of excerpt-

www.ingramcontent.com/pod-product-compliance
Lightning Source LLC
Chambersburg PA
CBHW061202170626
46809CB00003B/1206